Blood Legacy

PULSE 6

❧

kailin gow

Blood Legacy: Pulse 6

Blood Legacy (PULSE #6)
Published by THE EDGE
THE EDGE is an imprint of Sparklesoup Inc.
Copyright © 2011 Kailin Gow

For information, please contact:

THE EDGE at Sparklesoup
14252 Culver Dr. A732
Irvine, CA 92604
www.theEDGEbooks.com

kailin gow

First Edition.
Printed in the United States of America.

9781597480109

DEDICATION

This book series is dedicated to all the nameless volunteer blood donors, my doctor, and nurses at Las Colinas Medical Center in Texas who helped me pull through when I had suffered extreme blood loss, blacked out, and nearly hit my head on the floor. Your team gave me bags of blood for transfusion, which helped restore me to a level of safety.

My body craved the blood to keep alive, yet the thought of having to receive the blood from others because my own body couldn't generate it fast enough, made me empathize with vampires like Jaegar and Stuart.

When faced with death by blood loss, you realize how precious that blood in your veins and that beat in your heart are. Thank you blood donors around the world for providing this pulse for me and everyone who may at one point or another require your gift.

Sincerely,

Kailin

Prologue

The night was cold, and the moon was smooth above her, its milky whiteness making her pale skin even lighter. She looked down at her smooth, nearly-translucent hands and shuddered. Was this what she looked like now? She remembered when her flesh had been rosy with life, the first flush of its blood adding pink hues to her olive skin. But that had been another life. A life before her blood had begun its slow, dark hold upon her. Before the hunger started...

She looked down at her body. Still slender, still lithe – those muscles she had once so proudly honed through hours of early-morning runs still taut upon her bones. But she could see the change. She could feel it. In the beating of her blood. In the way her skin grew whiter than the stars above her. She wasn't human any longer. Not when she walked the night like this, intoxicated by the smell of blood all around her. Humans who had passed through this wood ages ago – hours or even days – the traces of whom still filled her with ravenous desire.

No, Kalina whispered to herself, gripping the wheel of the car. *No, this isn't me. I don't want this.* She hadn't been turned; there was no reason for her to feel this hunger, this vampire need. And yet she felt it, stronger than any thirst she had ever felt before. The craving to sink her teeth, newly-sharp, into someone else's skin, the desire to suck the blood from someone else's neck.

Please let this be a nightmare. Kalina closed her eyes. *Please don't let this be real.*

But it was real. She was driving through that now-familiar wood, on the path that ran between the Greystone Winery and her own home. If she could even call it a home. Hours before she had left Stuart alone in the house he had wanted to make hers, the house he had wanted to share with her. She had turned down his love, along with the life he wanted to make with her.

She had made him human. Her blood had spoken, decreed him her true love. And yet what her blood wanted, her heart and soul could not bring themselves to desire. Stuart had wanted a normal life: a normal *human* life. To attend seminary – seven centuries after he had first made up his mind to go – to get married, to have children. And as much as Kalina cared for him, she couldn't bring herself to submit to all that. At least, not yet. How could she force herself into a normal, human life when she *wasn't even human*?

She had turned Stuart, that much was clear. Unlike Jaegar, he showed no signs of turning back. But had she turned herself in the process.

There's got to be a cure. Kalina stepped on the gas. She had to get away, to get as far from Stuart as possible. She needed time. To think. To process things. To let herself wonder...

If Stuart wasn't her true love, then who was? Was it Octavius, the thought of whom still made her weak at the knees? Was it Jaegar?

Jaegar...

Blood Legacy: Pulse 6

She couldn't bear to think of him as he was the last time she saw him, with that pain so wide and palpable in his eyes. Seeing her turn his brother instead of him. Seeing her choose Stuart. How could she explain that her decision was born out of compassion, not love? She had wanted to save Stuart – not to spend her life with him! And yet Jaegar had fled into the night, never suspecting, never knowing that she loved him, too.

Stupid! Kalina pushed down on the brakes and stopped short in front of her old house. She rested her face on the steering wheel, closing her eyes. How had she let things get this out of control? She'd thought that she could handle it – balancing Stuart, Jaegar, and Octavius. Balancing her feelings. Her desires. But instead she was alone – Stuart sitting and mourning her loss at Greystone, Octavius off goodness-knew-where fighting Mal's troops, and Jaegar...

Gone.

She'd tried to do the right thing. She'd tried not to hurt anybody. She'd wanted so badly to give

Stuart the humanity he craved. And now all she'd managed to do was hurt the men she loved.

For she loved them all – all three of them. She knew that now. She'd never be able to truly choose just one. She loved Stuart's kindness, Octavius' strength, Jaegar's laugh. The moment she settled on one, the features and memories of the other two would come flooding into her brain.

But would this love leave her with none of them?

Kalina sighed as she fumbled with her keys, opening her door. Her eyes quickly adjusted to the darkness, and to her surprise she didn't even need to flick on the light. Another vampire skill, she supposed. Another proof that she was anything but normal. It had only been a few weeks since she'd last given this place a good look, but it felt like much longer. The place was no longer familiar to her in that same, comfortable way that it had been for eighteen years. She recognized it intellectually, but emotionally something was missing. The sense of *home.* This wasn't her home any longer. It was just a house – a house she had once lived in. A life she had once belonged to. But it wasn't hers anymore. Something had changed – not in the house, no, Kalina noted with a frown. That looked just as it always had done.

She had changed.

Kalina caught sight of the family portrait that she and Justin had always kept on the front hall table. It was one of the very few pictures that had ever been taken of the whole family together – a toddler Justin in her father's arms, a baby Kalina in the arms of her mother. The Calloway family. Kalina picked up the picture and fingered its frayed edges. Could she really have been that tanned, happy, healthy little baby in the photograph? Surrounded by such love, such warmth? Certainly her biological mother Max had never loved her that way – perhaps Max had grown to care for Kalina, with some measure of grudging respect, but Kalina had never seen in Max's eyes the warmth and joy exuding from the photograph of Joan Calloway.

"Mommy," she whispered, putting the photograph back on the table.

She trudged upstairs. She wanted to lie down, as she had done when she was a little girl, curl up with her favorite pillow and the blankets over her head. Perhaps then she could shut out the agony of the voices in her head – memories of Stuart, of Jaegar, of Octavius, even of Aaron...the voices that were almost as bad as the hunger. She'd put on her favorite records, the ones she used to listen to when she was little.

She'd be that happy, healthy little girl in the photograph, even if it was only for a second.

Yet as she opened the door to her bedroom, Kalina found that even her old bed no longer seemed safe to her. She couldn't look at it without thinking of the times she had kissed Stuart there, of the night Jaegar had spent there, of the time Octavius had come to her window in the middle of the night. She had feared him then – then, he had been the enemy – but even in the middle of her fear and contempt she had felt that visceral reaction to him, that stirring of desire. How could she look at her old room, trying to restore memories of a childhood before vampires?

Blood Legacy: Pulse 6

No, it was no use. There was no *before* any longer – she'd never be able to go back to that life.

She touched her bathrobe and remembered Octavius' soft caress. She remembered how her flesh had tingled beneath his firm, rough touch. She remembered the shimmer of the necklace he'd given her, how the cool diamonds felt against her flesh. She remembered how she had shuddered with desire, with longing for him. A desire which came over her again like a wave of sickness, sending her reeling. Where was Octavius now? Fighting vampires, most likely – off saving the world as he was always doing. Getting as far away from her as he could manage to go. Probably with Max, her mother – searching for the Carriers that Mal had hidden somewhere in Europe, hoping to find and save them before it was too late.

Kalina sighed. No matter how much she loved Octavius, he would never really be available to her. He had sworn to spend eternity fighting every last rogue vampire, refusing to turn human until every vampire he had turned became human before him.

He would never rest, never stop, never let himself break that sacred vow.

He would never let her truly love him.

Kalina sat down on the bed, and then her mind went next to Jaegar. Not the cocky, fun-loving Jaegar that she knew, but the terrifying, passionate Jaegar that had come to her when hopped up on Life's Blood, no longer willing to subsume his desire for her beneath a veneer of gentility. Trying to seduce her, trying to make her his – filling her with longing and terror mixed together.

A feeling she still couldn't shake.

And here, too, there were memories of Stuart – Stuart who had been willing to risk his life for her, who had been willing to risk his humanity. To fight Jaegar to the death – to save her...

Kalina shut her eyes, trying to will the memories away. So much had happened now – so much she'd never recover from, no matter how hard she tried. So much love. So much pain. She grew furious with herself – why couldn't she just *decide*? Why couldn't she just make her choice and be happy with it? She could have that normal life – just stick with Stuart, live a human life, go to Yale, get married to a good, kind man who loved her...

That was the choice her blood had made, after all.

But not her heart. Her heart had told her that Stuart wasn't the answer. Staying in the human world wasn't the answer – especially not when her lips had started to grow thirsty at the smell of human blood. There was some other destiny waiting for her. There had to be.

Suddenly, Kalina sat up, sniffing the air. Her blood began to prickle, her skin tingling. A familiar sensation – one she had come to know all too well. It meant that another Carrier was in the area.

A Carrier – in her house? She sprang to her feet. Had Max returned from Europe already?

"Max?" she called softly, tiptoeing towards her door.

The door opened, and Kalina gasped.

"*Justin?*"

Chapter 1

Kalina's mouth dropped wide open.

"Whom did you expect – the Queen of England?" Justin laughed. "Of course it's me. You think I don't keep this house pretty darn well locked up, considering all the dangers out there?" He strode into her room, blithely unaware of the look on her face. "What are you doing here? I thought you'd be spending the night at Stuart's? He's not here, is he?"

"No," Kalina shook her head quickly. "Listen, Justin, you didn't feel anything just now?" She looked him up and down, frantically checking for any signs of a change. But, other than looking slightly stronger and healthier, Justin seemed no more vampiric than he ever did. But her blood was burning, her heart beating with a frenzied beat. No, Kalina thought – this was *definitely* Life's Blood she was sensing. And it was definitely coming from him.

"Feel anything – like what?"

"Like...this heat, coming over you. This feeling in your blood – I can't explain it..."

Justin sat down next to her on the bed. "Kind of hot, you mean? Because I've been feeling a little weird – I just figured I was coming down with the flu..."

"Justin, listen to me. When you walked in right now, my blood did something weird. Something...like it recognized your blood, and I started to get all hot and flushed and my heart started beating really really fast and I *felt* something. Something I only feel when I'm around Max. Or another Carrier."

"I don't get it," Justin said. "You think Max is here?"

"She *is* here," Kalina said. "Or at least, a part of her is..."

Justin's eyes widened with understanding. "Her blood," he said, nodding. "When I was injured, she gave me her blood..."

"It worked, didn't it? It healed you, but..."

"But now I have Life's Blood in me," Justin finished her sentence.

"Impossible," Kalina whispered. But she knew it wasn't impossible at all. Far from it. She shuddered. If Max had been able to turn Justin into a Carrier, that meant that he was in danger, too.

"I've never heard of a male Carrier before," said Kalina. "Max always made me think it was impossible."

"Who knows what Life's Blood is capable of doing?" said Justin. "Every time we think we understand it, it starts to surprise us."

Kalina flushed as she thought of her new vampiric hunger. Apparently her brand of Life's Blood was even more surprising than everyone else's. But she said nothing. Justin was nervous enough about being around vampires – the last thing he needed to hear was that his own sister wanted to eat him for lunch.

"That's just it," said Kalina. "We don't know what Life's Blood really is. We don't fully understand what it can and can't do. It's part of us now. Which is why I'm here. And not back at the Greystone Winery with Stuart."

"You mean you two...?"

"Uh huh," said Kalina. "I tried, Justin, I really did. But for goodness's sake, I'm *eighteen*. I can't get married. I can't have kids. I certainly can't settle down when there's Carriers out there who need saving. I don't care *what* Octavius said – it's my problem now, too."

"I'm sorry," Justin said after a pause. "I'd hoped..."

"What, that I'd stay with Stuart?" Kalina couldn't help snapping. "Sorry, I know you liked him and all..."

"Not that," said Justin. "I just meant that I'd hoped you'd be happy. Whomever you chose. I hoped that choosing somebody, that getting away from those vampires – that things would start to get easy for you again."

"They won't," said Kalina. "They never will, Justin. I know that now. I told Stuart that I cared for him, that I *must* have loved him or I wouldn't have been able to turn him. But that it wasn't enough. My heart was telling me no."

"How did he take it?"

"Not great," Kalina admitted. "But not badly, either. I mean – he wants to stay here, to study to become a minister, to live this normal happy life. And I gave him a chance to do that. Just...not with me."

"He really loved you," Justin said.

"I know," Kalina looked down quickly. "But that turned out not to be enough. And anyway, Justin – when we were in China, at that old doctor's house. I found something. This box – it was like it was calling to me or something. But I can't open it. It's got some sort of lock on it – and I get the sense it's not the sort of box I'm supposed to smash open with a hammer. I think Max or Octavius might know how to get it open – or what it is."

"But who knows where they are?" Justin sighed. "Last time we saw them even *they* didn't know where they were going. Who knows if they've got any leads on the Carriers by now? They can't come all the way out here just to look at a box – time's running out for those girls. Who knows how much food or water Mal left them with? If someone doesn't find them soon, they'll die!"

"Which is why I'm not suggesting they come out here," said Kalina. "I'm suggesting we go *there*. I want to leave tonight, Justin." It wasn't just the box, Kalina knew. She had to get away from this town, away from all these memories of her past...a past that didn't want her any longer. "I can fly to Ulan Batuur and find out where Octavius has gone to from there. Or I can try to reach him with telepathy..."

"Can't you reach Jaegar?" Justin asked, but Kalina said nothing, flushing suddenly. She hadn't been able to reach Jaegar telepathically since Stuart had turned – it was clear to her that Jaegar had chosen to cut off their communication. Now she didn't even know where he was...

"Listen, Justin," Kalina began. "I just want you to know that I know that this is something I have to do alone. I've risked your life too many times, and it's not something I want to do again..."

"Nonsense," said Justin. "You're my little sister, and where you go, I go. Besides, if what you say is true, and if I have Life's Blood in me, then I'm much safer being around a girl who knows her way around a stake than sitting here on my own..."

"You have a point," Kalina admitted. But she hated the idea of bringing Justin any closer to danger than he was already. Already she had nearly lost him, and the thought of losing him for good made her feel nauseous.

"Come on, sis," Justin said. "We have to go. I only have one condition for you."

"What's that?"

"We fly the *normal* way. Cramped seats. Uncomfortable twelve-hour flights. I love you, but I do *not* want you doing that vampire-drag with me half-way across the ocean. Makes me sick."

"Careful," said Kalina. "Now that you have Life's Blood in you, who knows? You might be able to start flying yourself."

Justin looked a little green at the thought. "I hope not, sis," he said, "because I'm pretty happy with normalcy."

They packed their bags, and as dawn was setting out over the horizon, they headed downstairs, suitcases in tow. Crickets had just finished their night song; crows were welcoming the morning. Kalina breathed a sigh of relief. They were going – she'd get away from this town, away from Stuart, away from her feelings of confusion. Anything was better, she thought, than being near Stuart, seeing how much she had hurt him. She needed time to cope with her decision.

But then she sensed him – her smell preceding her sight. She sniffed the air, and hunger flooded through her. Stuart's car was pulling into the driveway, stopping so short that the tires screeched.

"Hey, slow down!" Justin called out.

Stuart emerged from the car. Kalina rushed to him, only to see that he was bleeding profusely from a gash on his right shoulder. Before she could think about what she was doing, Kalina was at his side – speeding like lightning across the front yard – her mouth upon his wound. The taste of him, the feeling of his blood upon her tongue, was unlike anything she had ever tasted before; her skin was warm with desire, her whole body trembling with pleasure.

Stuart was moaning softly as her fangs entered his skin, his eyes closed and his eyelids fluttering with longing.

"Kalina, what the *hell*?" Justin was standing at the doorway.

Kalina came back to herself. She stepped away in shock, covering her mouth as her cheeks blushed bright red with shame.

"I'm sorry," she whispered. "I don't know what just happened. I saw the blood and I wanted to..." She wiped her lips with the back of her hand, looking with horror as bright red streaks came away on her knuckles.

"Did you just..." Justin was gaping at her.

"I don't want to talk about it," Kalina snapped.

"But you just..."

"It's a thing."

"You're not a..."

"No!"

"But you just..."

"I don't want to talk about it, okay?" Kalina couldn't help shouting at Justin. Not being able to control her bloodlust was embarrassing enough, but to lose control like that in front of *Justin?* Stuart, meanwhile, was looking at her with adoration. Her instincts towards him had only made him love her more. How could she bear such kindness? And yet, as she stared at him, her former love was mingled with her present hunger. She had made her decision – she didn't want to be with Stuart. But as long as he was before her, his blood so sweet, like chocolate or fine wine, how could she remember that choice? She wanted nothing more than to sink her teeth into him, to devour him whole.

She looked intently at the floor. "I wanted to heal you," she said glumly.

"It's okay," said Stuart. "I've been there. I've felt that hunger before. Whatever happened to you – you're not a vampire. You're fine in sunlight, for starters. It's probably just some weird Life's Blood effect – you can still eat human food, right?"

Kalina nodded. Cheeseburgers weren't quite as tasty as they had been a year ago, but she could certainly force them down.

"Then it's probably not a full-force craving. Just a weird holdover from the vampire part of you.

But that doesn't mean it isn't hard..." Stuart patted her hand.

"Stuart, you came just in time to say goodbye." Kalina took a deep breath. She hated to hurt him more than she had to. "I'm going back. To Europe, I mean. Or Asia. Wherever Octavius and Max are. This...thing that's happening to me – with the hunger and all. I need to deal with it, and I need to deal with what's going on."

"I see." She could see the flicker of disappointment in Stuart's eyes. Had he been hoping that she'd take him back. "Then that's what you have to do."

He took a step back, and Kalina's blush spread across her face.

How could she bear causing him so much pain?

Chapter 2

Kalina had managed to regain her self-control. While she couldn't tear her eyes away from Stuart's pulsing, gaping wound, she had at least managed to keep her fangs firmly within her mouth. She looked down at the ground as intently as she could, not wanting either Stuart or Justin to see the slight protrusion of her lips where the fangs now poked out.

"You're not going to eat *me*, are you?" Justin was asking in a small voice. "I mean, this hunger you have..."

"I think it's only for turned vampires," Kalina lied. "Definitely not for you." This was mostly true – to her relief, Justin's blood smelled far less delicious to her than Stuart's. If she was going to want to eat somebody, she reasoned, at least that somebody wasn't her brother. "But Stuart, your wound..." She made a concerted effort not to let herself look at it directly. "How did you get it? Are you injured?"

Stuart said nothing at first, but only coughed and colored slightly.

"Stuart, what is it?" Kalina pressed.

Stuart sighed. "It looks like being a human again after so many years has a couple of disadvantages. One of them being that I can't fight off vampires as easily as I used to."

"You were attacked?" Kalina raised an eyebrow. She'd heard of resentful vampires seeking out the ones turned human by Life's Blood. Back when the Consortium was fully operational, Octavius had been able to sort out former Carriers and their vampire loves with new lives, new identities, hidden from the possibility of vampire attack. But she and Stuart had no such luxury.

"It was...strange," said Stuart slowly. "Feeling like that. Like prey. I was so used to feeling powerful, feeling strong. Preying on others. Now, for the first time, I know what it feels like to be hunted like an animal."

Kalina slipped her hand in his. "Now we both know what it feels like," she said. "To be in the other one's shoes."

"I fought them off as well as I could," said Stuart. "I may not have vampire skills, but I have six hundred years of experience. And that counted for something – although I didn't quite get away unscathed."

"I'm sorry," Kalina said. "I shouldn't have left you behind. I should have made sure you were safe."

"You couldn't have known," said Stuart softly. "Even I didn't expect it. I suppose I thought once you and I...well..." he flushed pink, "Once your blood lost its power to turn vampires, I imagined it wouldn't have quite a strong scent – fewer vampires would pick up on it. But as long as you're..."

Kalina sighed. She hated the idea that her virginity was implicitly tied into the scent of her blood – that every one of the lascivious vampires who came to try to taste her could *smell* whether or not she'd had sex. The idea disgusted her. She didn't want to give up her power to turn vampires, but she wasn't sure she liked the rules of this particular deal.

Clearly whoever created Life's Blood had quite an antiquated view of women, she scowled.

"I guess I still smell like fresh meat," Kalina sighed. "I swear, at this point I'm almost ready to just get it over with so vampires stop sniffing around me like..."

She looked up at Stuart and Justin, who were staring at her with shocked faces. "Never mind."

"It wouldn't matter, anyhow," said Stuart. "I smell of you now. The Life's Blood that you gave me is in my blood. Your lingering scent is enough for any vampire to track me down."

"Well, we can't leave you alone..." Justin strode over and patted Stuart on the shoulder. "You need protection. And you know, I'm a Carrier now." He stuck his chest out proudly. "Not a real one, of course – but Max put her Life's Blood in me."

Stuart instinctively sniffed the air, then stopped, confused. "I can't smell it anymore," he admitted. "You just smell like dirty laundry to me."

Kalina bit back a small smile.

Blood Legacy: Pulse 6

"Can we book another ticket, Kal?" Justin turned to Kalina. "Take him with us? He'll be safe there."

Kalina hesitated a moment before answering. She knew as well as Justin did that they couldn't just leave Stuart alone – not if he was still a target for vampires looking to drain him of the few drops of Life's Blood he had in his system. But she'd been so looking forward to a fresh start – to getting away from the confusion that dulled her brain and yet heightened her senses. She'd needed time away from Stuart – to think, to come to terms with herself. She hated this physical attraction to him – the sheer force of her desire of his blood – that mingled with her knowledge, deep down, that she could not love him the way he deserved to be loved. The knowledge of her heart warring with the knowledge of her blood.

But that, it seemed, was not to be. "Of course we can," said Kalina, gritting her teeth. "But what about your dreams, Stuart? What about seminary? Staying here?"

"It's not safe," said Stuart, "and in any case – whatever you're doing, I can't not be a part of it.

I...care for you too much to let you risk your life without my help." His voice was shaking, and Kalina's heart ached for it. It was so clear that he loved her, even now; the force of his adoration floored her. How could she bear it? This longing, this desire...how could she bear the guilt of not being able to love him in return? Oh, why couldn't she just be *normal*, settle into normalcy, forget Jaegar, forget Octavius, forget the desires that scrambled her brain and set her blood afire.

"Book a ticket?" Stuart raised an eyebrow. "But why ever would you do that? We can take my jet."

"What?!" Justin nearly leaped out of his skin. "Private jet."

"It's amazing what a few-hundred-year-old investments can do. That's a *lot* of time to collect interest." Stuart grinned modestly. "I'm lucky enough to be able to live out the remainder of my days with a small fortune – well, a large fortune, rather. I've never wanted to spend it before – after all, when you're supposed to be alive for all eternity, you want to make sure you don't run out, so I've been living on the investment income. But now I probably haven't got more than eighty or ninety years ahead of me – if that – so I might as well get to spending it!"

"It would appear that Stuart and Jaegar bought up some cheap property when they first arrived in America almost two hundred years ago," said Kalina to Justin. "Bought it for almost nothing at the time. Now, of course, that property happens to be located in New York City..."

Justin's eyes opened wide. "How come Jaegar never told us about the jet? We had to fly commercial last time we went to Mongolia."

Stuart couldn't resist a smile. "Being the boring, organized one has its advantages. Jaegar spent all of his share of the profits on women and luxury hotel rooms. Me, I invested wisely. I've been running the business for years." He couldn't help turning to Kalina. "It's not all bad being a nice guy," he said. "We get things done." He took Kalina's hand in his. "My sweet," he said, "I may not be a vampire any longer, but I hate the idea that I might be useless to you. I want to do whatever I can to make you happy, and that means putting my resources at your disposal Physical, financial, or otherwise. Whatever you need to make your life work – I'm here."

Justin pulled out his phone, his fingers twiddling furiously. "So I'll just cancel those economy class tickets, shall I? I wonder if they do full refunds..." He went over to Stuart. "Well, I can't say I'd have minded having *you* for a brother-in-law! Do you *know* the interest rates on my student loans?"

"Justin!" Kalina turned bright red. She knew Justin was just trying to lighten an awkward situation, but his making light of her romantic indecision made her embarrassed. It was hard enough having to make these decisions without being constantly reminded of them.

"It would have been nice," Stuart conceded. He did not look at Kalina.

"He was always my favorite, sis," said Justin blithely, completely oblivious to the fact that his words made Kalina want the floor to open up and swallow her whole. "You can't beat a total gentleman who's willing to charter you out on a private jet."

"Guess you can't!" Kalina rolled her eyes. She loved her brother, but he sure could be clueless when it came to matters of tact.

"Protecting you, standing by you – even cooking for you! Hell, I *enjoyed* those meals. I hope you still cook, Stuart.'

"Justin..." Kalina's voice sounded a warning note.

"I'll still cook for you," Stuart was responding with a genial smile.

"I feel a certain sympathy for you, Stuart," said Justin. "I know what it's like to be the nice guy."

"From one nice guy to another," Stuart slapped Justin on the shoulder, "I thank you."

"I *get* it, Justin!" Kalina couldn't stop herself from shouting, her cheeks turning bright crimson. She was about to say, "Apparently I picked the wrong brother. Got it. Everybody should just *move the hell on!*"

She stopped herself before the hurtful words came out, covering her mouth with her hands. She had never lost her temper like this before – especially not with Justin or with one of the men she loved.

Apparently this new vampire nature came with a new vampire temper.

"Uh, sorry," she said.

She'd have to learn to control that, too. A few months ago, she'd have laughed off Justin's jokes as the lame attempt at lightening the mood they were. But things were different now. She felt a deep guilt at not being able to love Stuart the way he loved her – and being reminded of just how good he was, just how kind, how special, only made everything harder. Why couldn't she just love him – just settle down and stay with him and forget the way Jaegar made her tremble, the way Octavius made her swoon.

Stuart walked them over to his car. "The Rutherford Airfield is only a few minute's drive from here," he said. His face was happier than Kalina had ever seen it. Although in his eyes she could still discern the sadness he felt at her loss, Stuart nevertheless seemed more full of genuine joy as a human than he had ever been as a vampire. That sad, haunted look in his eyes – the look of agony as he constantly struggled to repress his desires, to forget what he had done – had vanished.

He bowed slightly, a smile spreading over his face. "My chariot awaits, m'lady." It was just a joke, but as he spoke Kalina saw through the traces of the modern-day Stuart she had come to know. This was the human Stuart – hundreds of years old – once a valiant knight on the battlefields of Medieval England. Years of vampire savagery had not made him forget the chivalry of his age; he was no less noble now than he had been then.

Kalina smiled back. Whether or not he was her true love, she knew, she was sure lucky to have him in her life.

"Hand me down, m'lord," she teased back, her heart lightening just a little. She would always care for Stuart, she knew. She couldn't write him out of her life just yet.

Chapter 3

❧

"*Wow!*" Justin's mouth hung agape as they looked around the luxurious private jet. It was larger than any jet Kalina had ever seen, with plush leather seating and even a private sleeping compartment. Stuart had filled the mini-bar full to bursting with fine wines and exquisite delicacies – a hunger born out of centuries of not eating human food – and he immediately started tearing into an enormous plate of French cheese, Belgian chocolates, and Italian grapes. "When I was growing up," Stuart explained, "we had bread and perhaps meat a few times a year – if we were lucky. Food was something to sustain us, not something to *enjoy*. And then I was turned... But now, it's incredible! All these varieties of food – all these options. I could eat meat every day if I wanted! Well, not on Fridays, of course..."

Blood Legacy: Pulse 6

"Most Christians don't fast on Fridays anymore," said Justin. "Even Mom and Dad didn't, and they were pretty religious."

"Not...fast on Fridays?" Stuart looked confused. "Then..."

"A lot's changed since you were last human, my dear Stuart," said Justin. "But if you want to explore the world's culinary pleasures on your private jet, then I'm more than happy to serve as a tour guide....maybe we'll stop in France, first. Pick up a few baguettes, some of those delicious sausages..."

"Justin!" Kalina laughed. "We can't stop in France – we've got somewhere to *be*. This is a mission, not a luxury cruise."

The flight attendant, a buxom redhead, came over to serve Kalina and Justin drinks. But when Stuart requested a glass of champagne, her eyes widened.

"Champagne?" she whispered, her eyes looking Stuart up and down with seductive need. "But, sir, you always used to..." Her eyes went instinctively to her pale, white wrist, where Kalina could discern faded puncture marks. Kalina swallowed down her jealousy.

"Not anymore, Helena," Stuart smiled, evidently oblivious to Helena's disappointment. "Now I will eat and drink like a man – and dine with my friends."

Helena looked confused. "I *see*, sir."

She strode off in what Kalina noted a small resemblance to a huff.

"Well," Stuart turned to Kalina, lightly touching her face with his soft fingers. "My love, this plane is at your command. What is your heart's desire? Where shall I take you?"

Kalina blushed bright red. Was Stuart still trying to win her back? Was that why he was doing all of this – impressing her with his private plane, his French champagne, his fine chocolates? Was he trying to prove to her that he was still the right man for her?

It wouldn't work, she told herself. She had made her choice; now it was only fair to stick to it. Still, it was nice to see this Stuart again - glimpses of the romantic, happy Stuart she had known only in brief moments, like on the night of Kalina's senior prom, when he trusted himself enough to let go of his inhibitions and give himself over to passion. Now he no longer needed to fear that his passion would come with a price: if anything, he needed to worry about *her* hunger for him. And so Stuart was now a happier, better version of himself – still, as ever, a smooth and chivalrous gentleman, but no longer afraid of the passion that lay within.

"Where to?" Kalina ignored Stuart's flirtations for a moment, finding it easier to instead focus on the practical. The practical didn't demand so much of her heat. "When Mal and...that *woman* were talking..." Remembering cruel, mocking Olga made Kalina angry, and she couldn't bear to say her name. "They said that the Carriers were hidden all over – but that they'd been the ones to hide them. Olga was in charge of taking care of them, watching over them, until they..." Kalina made a face of disgust. "Ripened. That was the word she used." The full force of the word's meaning struck her. These little girls – some as young as ten years old – were being groomed to become playthings to vampires. She knew vampires were capable of great depravity – hell, she had seen plenty of it – but this was beyond the pale.

"If Olga was working in Russia, maybe she hid the vampires there. Mal probably didn't want her to stay in China, maybe he intended for her to go back to Russia to take care of them?"

"Can't you find out?" Justin asked. "Without a firm lead – even if we knew to go to Russia, it's a pretty darn big place. Can't you ask...wait, Stuart! You still have a telepathic connection with Max, don't you?"

Stuart shook his head, his ears turning pink. "I used to," he admitted. "But not anymore. Ever since Kalina turned me, the only connection I have is with her. Her Life's Blood superseded whatever Max put in me – it was stronger. And our connection is better. Now Kalina can read my mind."

No, Kalina cried inwardly. She wouldn't dare let herself read Stuart's mind. She couldn't let herself into his brain – couldn't deal with the full force of what she knew he was feeling deep down. *Kalina,* she heard him cry from deep within his soul, unable to bear the full force of his words. *Kalina, I love you still. I want you still.*

No, she couldn't bear to listen to those words; she couldn't bear his love! Not when she was so unsure of herself. Had she been too hasty in giving him up? She had thought, when she told him that she couldn't be with him, that she couldn't give herself to him and give up that power to turn other vampires, that they had been so different, that they had such different goals, different dreams. But here he was – willing to fight for her, to give up his dreams of peace, of seminary and living a quiet life at the vineyard – willing to do whatever she wanted, whatever she needed. All for her. All to be with her. All in the off chance that she would want to be with him.

Stuart was looking at her expectantly. She didn't even need to read his mind to know what he was thinking; it was all in his eyes. He loved her so much – so much that it killed her.

She let her mind open to his – just wide enough to pass her message through without Justin hearing it. *Stuart, you know I still have feelings for you, I still care for you very much, but...*

I know, Kalina. You turned me. You made me human. How could you do that if you didn't truly love me, deep down inside you? You must know that, beneath your fears, your duty to the Carriers, you want to be with me.

But I don't want what you want, Stuart. You know what I have to do. Kalina looked down quickly, anxious that Justin not see the tears forming in her eyes. He was blithely oblivious, absorbed in the vast variety of games he could play on the seat's computer screen.

I thought you wanted the same, Stuart was telepathing back to her. *You wanted to go to Yale. You wanted all that. You wanted a normal life. You wanted to be normal.*

I thought I did. I never lied to you Stuart.

But something changed.

Yes, Kalina thought to herself. Something *had* changed. She had changed. She no longer wanted to be normal. She may not have liked being vampire fodder – but she didn't want to deny herself her identity, either. She had the opportunity to fight for the cause, to help re-form the Consortium, to save the Carriers. How could she selfishly turn all that down just to live a life of stability and normalcy?

Yes, something changed.

Stuart came over to her seat, sitting next to her. She could feel his warmth, his touch. He took hold of her hand and lifted it to his lips.

"I'll help you through it, Kalina," he whispered softly. She could feel his hot breath tickling her ears. He looked down. "I've changed, too. You've changed all our lives now."

"Did you get it?" Justin looked up suddenly.

"Get what?" Kalina said quickly, blushing.

"Any sort of a mind-read from Max or Octavius? Any hint about where they might be?"

Kalina shook her head. "No," she said glumly. But the mention of Octavius made her heart ache with a slow pang. She had not heard from him since he had bidden her farewell, giving her his blessing to go ride off into the sunset with Stuart. Perhaps he thought it was better this way – to let her forget him, to lead another life instead. But she couldn't bear that. She couldn't bear to lose him too. Had he chosen to sever their telepathic connection, as Jaegar had done – turned his back on her forever? No, Octavius had promised that he would always be there when she needed him. Well, she needed him right now.

Octavius! Kalina called, her whole body aching for the tingle of his touch. *Octavius – are you there?*

But there was no response.

"If the only lead we have is Russia," Stuart was saying, "I'll tell the pilot to go to St. Petersburg first. Even if we don't know where Olga was, we'll probably run into some Russian vamps who might be able to give us a few leads."

"But..." Kalina sighed. How could Octavius be ignoring her? He'd certainly never ignored her before.

And then she heard his voice, echoing throughout her brain. So soft, so reassuring. So good. As smooth and sweet as honey.

Kalina?

Chapter 4

Octavius! A smile spread across Kalina's face – a joy so sudden, so overwhelming, that Stuart looked up at her with jealous concern. *Octavius, is it really you?*

What's going on? You're on a plane – but where are you going? I thought you and Stuart had already...

No – no...Octavius, where are you?

I can't talk long. We're heading into the mountains. It'll be a while...

Where are you? What mountains? Her heart was beating so fast now – the closer she got to him, the more she wanted him. Her whole body was aching for him, her longing so palpable that she could barely breathe.

We're in Switzerland, heading into the Alps. We got a lead from one of Olga's offspring...

"Head to Geneva!" Kalina called out to Stuart. "Tell the pilot to go straight to Geneva – no stopping."

What are you doing, Kalina? You can't come to us – it's too dangerous for humans.

Max is human! Kalina couldn't resist the jealousy. *She can come with you. Why can't I?*

She's a Carrier.

I'm a Carrier!

It's different. She's more experienced than you are. She's been fighting for longer, I'm not worried about her.

You don't have to worry about me.

I always worry about you. She could hear how his voice was still tinged with regret. And yet he still thought she was with Stuart. Still thought that she loved him. How *could* she love him – when her feelings for Octavius were still this strong? Nothing had changed. She still wanted him through and through.

Where is this place?

Is Stuart with you? Kalina thought she could detect jealousy in his voice.

Yes, she admitted.

Blood Legacy: Pulse 6

Ah. She could sense his pain. *Then ask him. He'll know where it is. The Devil's Mouth.*

The Devil's mouth, where is that?

Ask Stuart...

But Stuart and I...

But it was too late. Octavius' voice had faded away.

"What is it?" Stuart rushed over to her. Kalina was shaking, her pale skin turned dark crimson by the force of her love.

"Oh, no..." she whispered. How did Octavius still have that effect on her – even now he could reduce her to a quivering gale of desire?

"What is it? Is everything all right? Is somebody hurt?|

"No, no..." Kalina shook her head. "Everything's fine...I heard from Octavius. He's okay – he and Max both. But he told me where they were going. He said that he knew where the Carriers were – or thought he did. Somewhere called the Devil's Mouth. He told me you'd know where that is, Stuart?"

Stuart furrowed his brow.

"Yes," he said. "You spoke to him just now?" Now it was Stuart's turn to be jealous. It was as plain as day the effect Octavius still had on her – Stuart had to know that Kalina still had such clear feelings for him. "Kalina, you're trembling."

"It's nothing." She waved away his concern, not wanting him to see. "The Devil's Mouth – you know where that is?"

"It's in Switzerland by the French border," said Stuart. "It's a dangerous place – lots of supernatural activity going on there. Not somewhere you want to go for a skiing holiday. We can't land in the mountains – the plane's not equipped for that. But there's a private hangar a few hour's drive from the Mouth. Mostly used by celebrities who want to go skiing in the Alps without being seen. But we're not going on a holiday, are we?"

The whole plane journey seemed tortuously long to Kalina. She couldn't stand the waiting – knowing Octavius was on the other end, knowing that she wanted him so badly still...

If she had thought human hormones were difficult to deal with, vampire hormones were a million times worse. The desire of her blood was sending her in a hundred different directions – one minute she wanted to have sex with Stuart, the next minute she wanted to eat him! One minute she was feeling love for Stuart – the next Octavius was turning her to jelly! No wonder vampires were so promiscuous, she thought – vampire hunger for flesh was almost as bad as vampire hunger for blood.

As they descended, Kalina caught a flash of the white, snowy mountains out her window. How savage they looked – their untrodden carpeted whiteness so virgin, so untouched. These mountains were remote and dangerous enough that even the most hardened trekker avoided them – certainly there were no ski lodges clustered around the bases, as there were on the smaller mountains. Kalina felt the familiar thrill – terror and excitement – of danger. It had become like a drug to her, Kalina felt – the drug of desire.

Stuart started shivering as soon as they left the plane. They had come from California, after all, and although they'd brought sweaters and a change of clothes they hadn't planned on going straight into the middle of a cold snowstorm. Justin and Kalina huddled together, sharing Justin's oversized college sweatshirt between the two of them, their two heads poking out of the massive neck. But Stuart – evidently unused to the less powerful side of his human natures – was shaking heavily, his lips turning blue before they even reached the airport.

"We need to stay somewhere for the night," said Justin. "Not least so we can get some new clothes in town. Californian weather this is not!"

"I know a small inn near here," said Stuart. "L'Auberge des Escaliers – it's a lovely little place. And their roaring fire sounds very good right about now."

Of course, as Kalina quickly discovered, what Stuart called a "small inn" was in fact a luxury boutique hotel, its elegance taking the form of pseudo-rustic charm rather than cosmopolitan flair. Kalina gasped as she entered – ornately carved wooden walls stood over thick rugs: bearskin and sheepskin alike. A warm fire was blazing in the fireplace, and Stuart gratefully rushed over to warm up, rubbing his hands against the flame.

Blood Legacy: Pulse 6

"Is the Empress Suite available for tonight?" he asked the receptionist, who had come over to greet them.

"The Empress Suite!" The receptionist looked impressed. "Yes, I believe so, Mr...."

"Greystone," said Stuart lightly.

"Mr. *Greystone!*" Now the woman looked even more impressed. "I've heard your name mentioned. You're one of our most valued customers. You'd like to book the Empress Suite for tonight?"

"Only for Miss Calloway," said Stuart. "Justin and I will take the King Suite if it's available."

"Of course, Mr. Greystone," nodded the receptionist deferentially.

Kalina was glad to have some time to rest, freshen up, and sink into an extraordinary warm bath – from which she could see a view of the stunning Alps peaks out of the window – but she was somewhat awed by the atmosphere. Dinner was to be served at eight-o-clock sharp, and she had a feeling her jeans, very slightly muddied from the California autumn, wasn't going to cut it. She went back to her suitcase, looking in frustration for something that wasn't torn or designed to be worn while slaughtering rogue vampires.

"Looking for something to wear?" Stuart knocked lightly at the door. "I had the concierge send someone to pop into town to grab you this."

"Stuart, it's beautiful!" Kalina took a layer of shimmering, lace-lined peach-colored fabric from Stuart's arms. It was the most beautiful dress she had ever seen.

"If I'm going to make the most of my fortune in this lifetime," Stuart smiled, "I'm going to spend it on the woman I love – on making her happy. I daresay I know your body well enough to guess your size." His penetrating eyes smoldered as he turned his gaze upon her.

That night at dinner, Kalina could feel the cool softness of expensive silk rustling tantalizingly against her pallid flesh. The dress made her feel more than beautiful – it made her feel sultry. Seductive. Elegant. Stuart, too, was dressed up, wearing a well-made cashmere sweater whose color brought out the brilliancy of his eyes. He sat so elegantly at the table, Kalina noted with a pang, ordering their initial drinks with such élan. He may not have been born an aristocrat in England, Kalina noted, but by now he had certainly learned to play the part, showering her and Justin with such luxury that she colored.

They finished their drinks and Justin went on ahead to the main dining room, anxious to delve into some fine Swiss fare, muttering something about fondue. Stuart held out his arm for Kalina.

"My lady?" He gave her a slow, beautiful smile.

She touched his arm as she slipped her own through it, and at his touch waves of shock ran through her. Desire took hold; immediately she caught a whiff of his blood, her entire body aflame with her longing for him. Her hair was standing on end; even the hairs on the back of her neck bristled. She wanted him, she knew – and she wanted him this second, wanted nothing more than to bury herself in his lithe, strong body. She could smell his blood and she wanted it – wanted to drink it, wanted to gulp it down in great, sweet mouthfuls...

She tried to hide it, but it was too late. A rosy blush spread over her features, and she gave Stuart a look filled with such longing that she could not even bear to hide her thoughts from him. She could feel his mind reaching into hers, anxious for telepathy.

Do you feel that?

They're all staring at you, he responded. *All the other guests here. Hollywood actresses – princesses from Monaco. All of them – jealous because they're not as beautiful as you.*

It's not that.

No, it isn't. The dress is beautiful. Your body is sublime. Your face…ethereal. But you're exuding a kind of magnetism I've only even seen vampires use before. Powers of seduction beyond any human's wildest dreams. They'll all want you – every last one. And I'm no exception.

He stepped in closer, and the intoxicating scent of his blood was overwhelming. She put out a hand to steady herself, her fingers connecting with his warm, taut flesh.

"Oh, Stuart," she whispered.

"Shall we go into dinner?" His eyes were dark and smoldering with desire. "Or do you prefer to go upstairs – order room service instead?" A slow, sultry smile spread across his face. His hands were tight and rough upon her waist.

"But Justin's already..." she protested weakly. "We can't just leave him there."

"Oh yes we can," Stuart said. "I know that look in your eyes, and I'll be damned if I let it pass without doing something about it. I don't know when you'll look like that at me again – I never know with you. You're a beautiful changeling, always so enigmatic, always changing your mind. Well, this time you won't change it. This time I want you and you want me, and I'm going to have you if it's the last thing I do."

And then they were kissing, Kalina luxuriating in her hunger for him as their lips met and fumbled for each other in their lusty starvation. Her desire was warm and dark and overtaking her; she wanted his blood, his flesh, all of him – she wanted to possess him fully, to make him hers, to make him *only* hers. This was not the desire she had known as a mere human – the simple hormonal flush that had made her cheeks turn petal-pink with longing. No, this was something else – something deeper – a side effect of the turn her Life's Blood had taken. This was a desire so deep that it had become a desperate need: she needed to feed upon him, to own him, to will him to do her bidding and give her that pleasure she had too long been waiting for...

And then they were in her room, pressed up against the stone walls, down on the warm carpet before the fire, her skin naked against the bearskin as she let him remove her dress, tearing the delicate peace lace. She tore his cashmere sweater from him, thrusting it from her, wanting nothing more than to press her face into his warmth, his sweat, the sheer virile *manliness* of him. She was so cold – so pale and so cold – and she wanted his blood to heat hers, his life to give life to hers...

They were all-but-naked, writhing, and ecstatic. He kissed the straps of her bra, slipping them from her shoulders, fingering their delicate black lace. She wanted him – she knew it now, with a knowledge deeper than any rationality or reason – she wanted him with the full-force hunger of her blood. It called to her; it directed her – it made her the slave of these veins, these arteries, this pump and pulse of desire. She was so close to surrendering, so close to making him surrender to her.

And then there came a knock at the door.

Immediately, deflated, Kalina lay back upon the rug, the spell broken. Suddenly her self-control came back to her, the hunger-spell that had been cast upon her slowly dissolving into nothingness. What had she been about to do? She had been so close? Her body still ached with longing as she slipped on her dressing gown – Stuart's eyes burning with need as he watched her slip the black silk around her shoulders – and opened the door. "Room service?" she began, rolling her eyes. "You can really come back later; we're perfectly happy to..."

She stopped short, clapping a hand on her mouth.

There, standing before her, was Molotov, rage sparkling in his cold, glimmering eyes. And standing with him, kicking uselessly as Molotov clutched him by the throat, slowly squeezing out the last traces of vitality, was Justin.

Chapter 5

"What are you doing here…" Kalina started shaking, fumbling in the folds of her dressing gown for the stake she had hidden there, the rubies she had been given in the mountains of Mongolia now firmly encrusted around the stake's edge. Stuart too had leaped to his feet, a stake in hand as he rushed to the threshold.

"You let him go right now!"

But Molotov only pushed his way into the room, keeping his back to the wall as he held Justin – still writhing and coughing out what screams he could from the choke-hold – up against his front.

"You think I'm afraid of those stakes?" Molotov gave them a sardonic smile. "I doubt you'll try to stake me, girl. After all, I'm using your precious brother here as a human shield. Stake me, and his soft human heart will turn to jelly at the stake's end long before it even touches *my* flesh. I know I almost killed him once before – I can still taste him. And he was delectable. Almost as delectable, as you!"

Justin coughed and spluttered out his words. "Please, Kalina, just do it! Don't let him hurt you..."

"I saw your face the last time your darling brother nearly expired in front of you. You looked so crushed, so heartbroken. It warmed me to see you thus. Perhaps we should repeat the incident – without the *deus ex machina* coming in to save your dear brother at the end. After all I haven't fed for a few days. And we ancient ones do tend to get so terribly cranky when we are forced to go unfed for a while. We may not require blood with the same furiousness as the younger vampires in our midst – but when there is fresh blood to be had..."

Molotov grinned, revealing yellowed, blood-stained teeth.

"I would not refuse such an offer – especially when it comes with the prospect of causing you such exquisite pain."

Kalina's heart began to pound faster. All the ruby-lined stakes in the world would do no good, she knew, if she couldn't save Justin. Had Molotov really outsmarted them again? Even if she could match him physically – which she wasn't altogether sure she could – she was still no match for his centuries of experience. He had strategized on many more battlefields than she had – and he had won all his battles. She gulped as she stared into Molotov's cold, unblinking eyes.

"Please let him go," she whispered, her voice quivering. She had almost lost Justin once, and it had nearly killed her. She knew she couldn't bear to go through all that again.

Molotov picked Justin up by the neck as easily as if Justin had been a rag doll. Kalina winced as she heard the crack of bone. If Molotov had wanted to, it would have been so easy for him to snap Justin's neck in two right then and there. She shuddered.

"Please," she whispered. "Not my brother."

"I'd consider letting him go," Molotov began smoothly. "Only..."

"Only what!" Stuart stepped forward, his broad chest still rippling with muscles in the firelight. "What do you want from her?"

Blood Legacy: Pulse 6

"Stuart, get back!" Kalina cried. Now that Stuart was human, she knew he wouldn't be able to protect her *or* Justin. She'd have to protect herself.

"Only you have taken so much from *me* already. You and your precious lover Octavius, your whore of a mother – you have taken so much of what was mine. My men. My village in Mongolia, from which I drew my feeding stock. My offspring Mal, and with it the knowledge of what he has done with the Carriers I invested so much time, so much money, so many men to find..."

"Justin has nothing to do with this battle!" Stuart shouted. "He is innocent. Let him go. Your quarrel is with us, not with him."

"How sweet," Molotov said in false honeyed tones. "You wish to save your whore's brother. Well, I am far from impressed." He spat upon the ground. "It is disgusting – you and your brother both. In love with your maker's lover. She belongs to him – he has marked her – can you not see it? It is against the laws of nature for an offspring to mate with the love of his sire – it is disgusting, against all law of vampire honor. But you and your brother are no better than beasts. Than humans! And you claim to know what innocence means. You know nothing of innocence, my dear Stuart. You, who once spread fear into the hearts of men and women, terror into the nightmares of children, when you were the Dark Knight. *Then* you knew what it was to be a vampire. *Then* you would have been useful to me. I could have rebuilt my army from vampires like who you were then. I could have peopled my crowd of minions with your sword. But instead, like the pitiful fool you are, you let your human-loving ways taint the purity of your vampire blood, and now you have paid the price. What are you now but a weak, sniveling human...?"

Kalina stepped in front of Stuart, placing her body between his and Molotov's. Justin might be a shield in front of Molotov, but she would shield Stuart in her turn.

"No, I can think of a worse punishment than death..." Molotov spat. In a flash he had bitten into his own wrist, blood gushing forth from the wound. He placed his bleeding flesh upon Justin's mouth, forcing mouthfuls of blood down his throat. It took a moment before Kalina realized what Molotov was about to do...

"Justin, *no!*" she cried, but it was too late. Justin had drunk vampire blood. And that meant...

In a flash Molotov snapped Justin's neck, the crunch of bone echoing throughout the room, sending Kalina's blood running cold. Justin's face went white; his eyes rolled back into his head. He slumped over, dead.

"No!" Kalina screamed, tears coming to her eyes. "No!" She rushed forward, her stake in hand, ready to plunge it deep into Molotov's chest. But Molotov was too quick for her. He was already halfway across the room, picking up Stuart, his fangs bared, his wound still ripe for feeding.

Ready to try to turn him, too.

Kalina rushed over to Justin, but she knew with a sinking feeling nothing could be done. Justin had no pulse. And he had drunk vampire blood. That meant only one thing. He was going to turn – and turn he would, with Molotov as his master...

Adrenaline coursed through her, along with a rage so great she could hardly bear it.

"Kalina, help!" Stuart was fending of Molotov with a broken chair, but Molotov was far stronger than he. "Use the stake!"

Kalina rushed forth, but Molotov stopped her, his hand easily finding her neck.

"This is my lucky day," Molotov sneered, holding her in one hand and Stuart in the other, effortlessly incapacitating both of them at once. "Three conquests in one day. Two new minions to call my own – and a girl who might have so many other uses. Uses I can only begin to think of sampling..."

Tears were streaming down Kalina's face as she thought of Justin, lying dead upon the floor. It didn't matter, she thought – she didn't mind dying, now. She couldn't live without Justin, without her big brother – she didn't want to live at all...

She closed her eyes.

"Not if we can help it!" Kalina's eyes flew back open as she looked to the owner of that familiar voice.

A voice that gave her hope.

Blood Legacy: Pulse 6

Octavius and Max strode through the doorway.

Chapter 6

Kalina's heart was pounding fast. Seeing Octavius still made her tingle – even in the midst of her fear, her sadness, being with him was the only thing she wanted. Her body arched towards him; the hairs on the back of her neck prickled. She could not let herself think about Justin – not now – she had to block it out, block out the pain. She closed her eyes and let Octavius' presence waft over her like some intoxicating scent, filling the empty spaces within her heart. He had come to save her! Her heart leaped. He had come for her, as he had promised – he would always be there for her – he loved her...

"Octavius," she whispered, looking up at him, wriggling against Molotov's iron grip. She could see him turn his dark eyes towards her, his gaze so full of love, of desire, his countenance frozen in fear not for his own life; for he knew that he could easily fight off Molotov, but for hers. In that instance, Octavius betrayed to Kalina all he felt. He could not push her away – he could not pretend he did not love her. His love was plain on his face, made visible by his fear for her.

I'll never doubt him again, Kalina thought, tears coming to her eyes as Molotov tightened his grip on her neck and lifted her higher into the air. She struggled, but it was to no avail. Her neck only bruised beneath the force.

"I'm glad you've arrived, Octavius," Molotov was saying with a sneer. "It means you've come in time to see *this*!"

"No!" Octavius' booming voice echoed around the chamber, but it was too late. Molotov was too quick for them. In an instant, he had pulled Kalina's neck to his mouth and sunk his fangs deep into her throat.

It was a sort of release, Kalina thought dreamily. Never before had she been attacked so viciously – never before had she been attacked with such an immediate attempt to drain and kill her. From the moment Molotov's fangs were within her bloodstream, she stopped struggling. She was paralyzed – sleepy, even. As if something soft and somnolent had been swaddled around her – as if she had bathed in a hot bath and drunk a nice glass of warm milk. Yes, she thought – it was just like resting. And how easy it was to rest. Especially when she was so tired. Her eyes half-closed; her neck lolled back. Why, dying wasn't so bad, she thought limply. She had been so afraid of it, and here she was, dying as if it was nothing at all! Now she understood how easy it was to be drained – why so many women ached to be bitten by vampires. It wasn't a bad feeling at all. Only a strange one – a pleasant paralysis, like what a fly must feel when caught in the web of a particularly benevolent spider.

She began to lose consciousness, her awareness of herself rapidly decreasing. Soon, she was thinking only of Octavius – his face was the last thing she saw as she lost consciousness. His kind, beautiful face – like marble or lime – chiseled out of the stones of Olympos themselves. His anguished stare at her – his eyes wide open – his love.

So, he really does love me, Kalina thought sleepily as she passed out.

Blood Legacy: Pulse 6

As she lost consciousness, Octavius and Max let out twin wails of agony, rushing forth with their stakes in hand.

"You let her go!" Max roared, her small body taking on all the power and swagger of a brave lioness. "You don't *dare* touch my daughter." She raised her stake and threw it directly at Molotov's face.

It missed, but only by a hair, and Molotov let out a scream as the ruby-lined stake cut through his right cheek.

Now it was Octavius' turn to raise his stake and attack.

Immediately Molotov was on the defensive, keeping Kalina in his teeth like a dog holding onto a rag toy as he dodged Octavius. Octavius threw another stake, and this time the stake flew true, hitting Molotov in the back just as Molotov flew through the open window. Another stake flew through the window, missing Kalina by near inches.

But Molotov knew he could not carry her and escape freely at the same time. With a roar of defiance, he let Kalina fall, flying off into the night more swiftly for her lack of weight.

And then she was falling – falling down the cliff-side, faster and faster. She came in and out of consciousness, aware only of the bitter cold of the outside world, of the snow cutting against her cheeks, of the chill, of how fast she was falling towards the earth. Was she dying? Was she dead? Justin was dead – she would not live without him. She *could not* live without him.

She closed her eyes once more, bracing for impact. Not long now – she wouldn't feel a thing...she would be brave...she wouldn't be afraid.

And then she heard a swish of air alongside her, heard the parachuting swoop of a cape. Strong, muscular arms were around her, arms that gave her strength, gave her a faint warm glow. Arms that pressed her against a broad chest that smelled of musk and night.

"What's going on?" Kalina murmured, no voice escaping her soft and now-bloodless lips.

But she wasn't falling any longer. Instead, she was flying upwards, soaring into the sky, held ever tighter by those pair of arms that clutched her as if she was the most precious thing in the world. She looked up, a faint smile spreading across her lips. The figure holding her so tightly, gripping her as if he would never let her go, was Octavius. His eyes were moist with unshed tears, and his face was full of longing for her. He was cradling her with such gentleness, even as the tightness of his grip left faint bruises on her skin. His face was looking down into hers, love shining through his eyes. Immediately Kalina felt safe. Warm. Protected. Somewhere out there, terrible things were happening: Justin was lying dead on the floor of the Au Berge before a blazing fire, Carriers were starving to death inside a hidden compound, but these things all seemed so very far away now. Kalina was with *him* – they were together – she was safe. She was loved.

"Octavius," she whispered softly. "What happened? I was falling." She was shaking from the cold, from the lack of blood.

"I caught you," his lips nudged against her ear, brushing it lightly and sending a shiver down her spine. "I'll always catch you, Kalina."

"But we were so high up...I fell so far..." She opened her eyes, dizzy as she looked about herself. They were surrounded by snow – snowflakes that glimmered in the full moonlight.

"Before you hit the ground, I caught you." He nuzzled her gently, pressing his lips to her dark, shining hair. Small flecks of snow were caught between the fine, silky strands – like a crown of stars in a dark night sky.

"Where are we?" They were at the bottom of an enormous mountain whose peak stretched all the way into, it seemed, the clouds.

"The hotel was at the top of this mountain," said Octavius. "We're all the way at the bottom."

Kalina shivered, but she didn't feel cold. How could she feel anything but safe when Octavius was around? He sat beneath a tall pine tree, pulling her into his lap. Kalina nuzzled into him, feeling his soft cashmere sweater against her skin.

"Oh, my Kal," Octavius smiled softly. "Don't you ever scare me like that again. You're okay – don't be scared. You're fine. But I was so frightened – so afraid, watching you die like that. Watching you come so close to dying. You shouldn't have come here, Kal. Why did you come?"

"I had to come..." she whispered. "I have to save them. The Carriers."

"You could have stayed in Rutherford," he whispered, his voice so soft and caressing. "You could have had a normal life. Stayed far away from vampires. Stayed with Stuart."

Kalina propped herself up on one elbow. She was still very weak from the loss of blood, and she was shaking. "You know I couldn't do that," she said. "I never could." Seeing Octavius now made her so much surer of it. She couldn't stop herself from reaching out, cupping his face. She half-expected him to recoil, as he so often did, forcing himself to withdraw from her, to stop loving her. But this time he did not turn away. He closed his eyes and luxuriated in the sensation of her caress. Now she could hear his thoughts, their telepathic connection stronger than ever it had been before. Crystal clear.

You still love me. Her heart could not contain its joy, even as it still ached and bled with sorrows.

How could I ever stop? Don't you know, Kalina – even if you chose another, I would never stop loving you.

Molotov...

"He's gone," said Octavius out loud. His voice was gruff. "He's fled now. But now he's a danger. No vampire has ever had quite so much of your blood before – and we know just how strong your blood can be. He may be resistant to the rubies now – I don't know. All I know is that he's likely gone out to turn vampires, to rebuild his army."

"He drank from me," the memory was hazy now, like a cloudy morning. "I almost died."

Octavius' eyes darkened at the thought. "If he'd had one more gulp of you," Octavius said gravely, "he would have drained you dead. And I...it would have killed me, too. I saw that when I saw him drain you. I saw what an effect you had on me. I saw my own weakness so palpable and plain in my love for you." And then he pulled her in for a kiss. Kalina gasped in surprise – Octavius had not initiated a kiss with her in so long, always letting her chase him, wait for him, want him... But this time it was his turn to give in to their desires; she felt his mouth upon hers, felt him share his longing with her, his loss and his love. It was the kiss she knew he had held back for so long – and yet would hold back no longer. She felt her heart respond to him and to his blood; she felt herself grow weak-kneed with desire. They were together, beneath the falling snow, their minds and bodies and souls and blood all twined at last in the dizzying sensation of that kiss.

She never wanted him to let go.

Chapter 7

As they broke apart, their bodies still aching to stay alongside each other, Kalina was shaking. Her body had never quivered like this – the cold of the snow mingling with the heat of her longing. She had never felt as close to Octavius as she did right now. But it was more than physical proximity that made her feel that way. Something was different. Her blood was prickling more than normal – it was responding to his blood in a way she had never seen before. Her skin seemed to glow at his touch; her eyes sparkled as she beheld him.

"It's so strange..." She sat up, her strength returning. "Molotov almost drained me. But now I feel...almost fine." She stretched out her hands, looking down on the blue veins, the milky white skin. "Whole again?"

"You were sick, Kalina," Octavius murmured. "You'd passed out. When we landed here, at the bottom of the mountain, you were about to die. And, my God, I would do anything to save you. Anything. You would have died – Molotov was gone, but you'd still lost so much blood. You were whiter than the snow banks. And I just thought to myself – I cannot live without her. I must save her. I would have asked, but there was no time. You were unconscious; your skin was freezing. I kissed you – I placed my hands all over you – but I couldn't warm you up. And so I did what I had to do."

Now Kalina understood. She looked into Octavius' eyes, her gaze cool but full of love. "You gave me your blood," she whispered. "Is that it?"

He nodded. "My love, I know the dangers of the act. I knew that it would make the connection between us stronger than ever. It would make your feelings worse for me than they already were. But it, too, would weaken my own resistance against you. It would make me love you more. And it has, my darling Kalina. I feared that you would die with my blood in you and turn – a fate worse than death, Kalina. But it was the only chance I had at saving you. And I was selfish. Willing to take that risk if it meant not losing you – just as I did for Stuart and Jaegar so many centuries before. It is my greatest weakness: I cannot bear to lose those I love. Perhaps I acted selfishly in doing so. But you did not die. You survived." His voice was low and warm, velvety in its richness. "And now our bond is stronger than ever."

"Then you wouldn't turn me," Kalina whispered. "If I wanted you to?" She didn't want to be a vampire – but she already suffered from the hunger pangs, the vampire cravings. How much worse could it be to be made immortal? If Octavius would never become human, then she longed to live out eternity with him, for she could not bear the thought of vanishing into mortality as he went along without her.

Octavius shook his head. "If I were in my right mind, no. But seeing you almost dead – it made me crazy. Made me reckless. I am sorry for that now."

"Don't apologize..." Kalina brought him in for another kiss. "I can feel the bond. It's stronger than ever before. I can feel it, Octavius. You can't hide from me any longer what you feel. Because now I feel it, too – and Octavius, it's strong. Our love is too strong. Your essence is in me now, Octavius. Your blood is in me. I can feel it running through my veins."

Octavius smiled a sad smile at her. "Then you know what it's been like, don't you? What torture it has been spending each moment away from you – when I want nothing in the world so badly as to spend the night with you, each day with you, wrap my arms around you in bed and never let go. And then I start to waver and quake – I start to doubt myself and the oath I have sworn..."

He sighed.

"Why do you have to be so noble, Octavius?" Kalina pressed her lips against his marble-white forehead. "Why can't you ever think of what *you* want?"

"I do think of it," said Octavius. "I think of it all the time. But I cannot act on it. Not when I have brought so many vampires into this world of suffering – so many of them have been staked, with no hope of regaining their humanity. And those that remain still suffer. When I have brought such cruelty into the world, I cannot live with myself unless I cast it out again. Someone has to act as I must act, Kalina. Or else this world that you and I inhabit will become a different world, one where the likes of Molotov and Mal, vampires with no regard for human or vampire life, will rule. And the humans who rule, too, will be likewise cruel and callous. Without people like you, Kalina. Without people who have taken the oath that I have taken."

"That doesn't make it any less hard," Kalina said. "It's one thing thinking about what you *ought* to do – it's another thing working up the strength to actually do it." She thought once more of Stuart, of Jaegar, of her uncontrollable urges, and she was ashamed. Here she was, giving into each compulsion, each need, freely moving from vampire to vampire as her urges took her – even while Octavius wanted nothing in the world more than he wanted her, and yet he was able to force himself to resist. She thought once more of Justin, and her lips began to quiver with the pain and shame of it. If she hadn't left Justin alone, if she hadn't gone off to give in to her lust with Stuart, would Justin still be alive right now? Her eyes began to well up with tears at the thought. "I can't stand it," she whispered. "I've been awful – such a fool. Why can't I be as strong as you are, Octavius?"

"But you are strong, my sweet." He was stroking her hair. "Kalina, my love, you are the strongest woman I have ever known."

Kalina shook her head. "Not strong enough. I have these...urges. These desires – and they're so strong I can't control them. One minute I'm in love with Jaegar, the next with Stuart – *always* with you – and my hunger and desire are so strong I can't resist them. No matter how hard I try."

Octavius smiled sadly. "So you have a compulsion that makes you give into your urges by making them ten times stronger than normal."

"I'm so selfish! I've hurt Jaegar, hurt Stuart, hurt everyone I love by not being able to resist any of you..."

"But Kalina – doesn't it sound familiar to you? Uncontrollable urges – burning needs..."

"I don't understand."

"We vampires suffer from hunger all the time. And in your Life's Blood you have vampire blood.

And that Life's Blood has given you an incredible capacity to love – but also the pain of desire that comes with it. In us, vampire blood gives us an urge to feed. But in you, the urges are largely different. But how could I – or any of us – blame you for being overwhelmed by your blood, when we have struggled with that same question for centuries? I will not lie – of course it hurts me to see you with Stuart, with Jaegar, even with...Aaron." Octavius went quiet at the mention of the youngest Greystone brother, long since staked into oblivion. "But I understand how it must be for you. I've been there. I remember waking up that first morning in Ostia, feeling the hunger, my teeth sinking into the neck of a servant girl, a friend of mine, a girl I cared for..." He sighed at the remembrance. "I know how hard it is to control your needs, my love. Your desires. And when someone is as beautiful, as irresistible as you – you could have your pick of anyone, man or vampire. Your struggle is a noble one – you and I are not so different. We both struggle with longings we cannot control. Perhaps that is why my heart waited so long to find you – two thousand years without love, and then the day I met you all that changed. Perhaps..." He sighed...

She leaned into him, closing her eyes. She could think of nothing to say – there was no need for speaking. He could hear all her thoughts – coursing through her brain. Her fear about Justin, her terror that he would wake up a vampire, turned into one of Molotov's minions. Her loss, her loneliness. And still, alongside it all – her love. Her brain was going wild – she could think of nothing but that sure refrain: *I love you,* her heart was saying, *I love you, I love you, I love you.*

"Why do I have to love you?" Kalina said at last out loud. "It would be so much easier if I didn't, if you weren't in my life. Then the choice wouldn't be so hard. I'm so in love with you – I feel I'll never be able to move on. And if as you say, this blood connects us more – it'll be worse now than ever. For both of us." Because she knew what she wanted, she could not have. The two of them could never be together – she would have to suffer her longing and loneliness in silence; she would have to bear losing him once more.

Octavius gave an ironic chuckle. "Fate, perhaps?" he said slowly. "Fate that has wrenched us apart, torn us apart over centuries, and yet which keeps thrusting us back together. Perhaps we should wait and see what Fate has in store for us this time?"

"It could be worse," said Kalina, shuddering. "What if it had been Molotov's blood? Already he's got to Justin..." Saying it out loud made it more real. Tears came to her eyes and froze into snowflake on her lashes. "But you'll be able to save him, won't you?" Octavius had always come through for her before – she had to believe that he would come through for us again. She had to believe there was hope for Justin. "You won't let him become a minion of Molotov's, would you?" Her lips were trembling, pale and blue with the cold.

"I don't know," Octavius whispered. "I wish I could tell you sweet words to make the pain go away, my sweet Kal, but I cannot bear to lie to you. I do not know what will happen to your brother. I can only wait – and hope – and have faith..."

"I'm praying for him," the droplet-snowflakes were falling fast down Kalina's nose, wetting her fingers. "Right now. Will you pray for him too?"

He squeezed her hand. "I will, my love."

"Then we have to go back," she leaned into him. "Find out what happened."

He nodded.

"Then I'm ready," Kalina stood up, swaying as she did so. She was still dizzy from the blood loss and the pain. "Let's go."

Chapter 8

The sun was beginning to spread its tendrils across the sky. Dragonish clouds of yellow and orange, purple and pink, were rising with the dawn. The air grew warmer as the moon faded away, and Kalina felt the sun glimmer upon her face. She looked up. The mountain was high above them, its peak so high up that she couldn't even make it out. Had she really fallen so far? She sighed. How could she bring herself to go back? To see Justin...

That would make it real. And she couldn't let it be real. She couldn't even say the words out loud to herself: Justin was dead. Molotov had fed him his blood. Justin would turn. No, it couldn't be true – it couldn't! It was all a bad dream, some terrible nightmare. Justin was safe at home, safe and sound in his bed, nothing was wrong...

Blood Legacy: Pulse 6

And if she hadn't left him in the dining room, if only she hadn't gone off with Stuart, if only she hadn't given into her lust.

"It's better if you get on my back," Octavius was saying, rubbing her back with his fingers. Her body tingled as he massaged her taut, tense shoulders; she melted into him. He knelt down before her, his broad muscular back welcoming her. She tentatively stepped onto his shoulders, curling her legs around his chest as she wrapped her arms around his neck. Their proximity galvanized her. Feeling Octavius' skin against hers, feeling his closeness, drove her mad. She wanted him; she wanted to melt into him. She wanted him to protect her, to make everything all right. She couldn't let herself think of Justin now; she couldn't bear it! She just wanted to close her eyes and breathe in Octavius' musky, intoxicating smell, press her nose against him chest and breathe him in. All of him. She felt his blood coursing through her, her whole body shaking with the force of her desire for him. He was inside her; his blood was inside her, enchanting her from inside out.

Stop torturing yourself, Kalina, she told herself. *Stop it – you'll only make it worse. You'll only get hurt.* But Kalina couldn't control it. Now that she was all the more certain of Octavius' love for her, her desire for him was stronger than ever. She wanted him to take her then and there – she wanted him to drive out her pain, her loss, to kiss her into oblivion and in his pleasure remove her agony. She wanted to forget about Justin, forget about him lying there, his skin cold and clammy, his pulse dead, waiting to rise again...

She just wanted to forget.

Now that Octavius' blood was in her, she could feel his desires all the more keenly. She knew what he wanted; she knew what she wanted. She could feel that every muscle in his body was straining not to fly away from the inn, fly away from the mountain, fly to some quiet cave or hidden castle and ravage her utterly. His muscles tightened beneath her, and she knew he was tensing with his desire for her. She could feel how much he wanted it – more than ever before. And it was becoming harder and harder for him to keep control. Not when he wanted so bad to lose it, to luxuriate in losing it.

Yes, she thought gratefully – she wanted him to lose control. She couldn't with Justin now, she couldn't deal with her loss, with any of it. She wanted Octavius to take her away – far away from this pain, this sadness, far away from her troubles. Just for an hour – just for a day – she needed to forget. Her body was trembling with pain. Justin! How could she have been so stupid, letting him die lie that – why hadn't she been stronger? Faster? Better.

How could she have failed?

No, she wouldn't think about that now. She would let her blood take hold of her; her blood would make her forget. She leaned into Octavius, tightening her thighs around his waist, luxuriating in the ripple of his hardened muscles beneath her taut legs. She nuzzled the back of his neck, letting her tongue linger on the brittle hairs that lined it. She sucked gently on his earlobe, giving herself over utterly to the pleasure of touching him, of being near him.

"Careful, you," Octavius' voice was ragged with desire. Yet beneath the hoarse wariness there was a certain playfulness that Kalina had never detected before. "I told you – my love – we have to get back. And if you keep doing that, I won't be able to fly."

"Octavius," Kalina said, urgently. "Vampires don't turn in the day, do that?"

"No, the next night after they've been bitten. Always the next night."

"Then, if Justin were to turn..."

"I see." There was a pause. "Yes, Kalina – he would not yet have turned. He would turn at sundown."

"Tonight?" Her voice quivered.

"Yes, tonight."

"I don't want to see him like that, Octavius," Kalina said in a small voice. "I don't want to see him lying there like that – knowing what's going to happen to him...oh, Octavius, he never wanted this! His biggest fear, you know? Being turned. He was so terrified of it – even when we thought he'd need to turn to protect me. He didn't want that. And I can't just *look* at him – I can't wait."

Blood Legacy: Pulse 6

"You'll need your strength tonight," said Octavius. "My love – it will be difficult for you. I know that. You will have to see things that strike you to the core. You will have to make a choice. What you see tonight will be your brother, and yet not your brother. He will know you and yet he will not know you. I can tell you now that even in vampires, the shadow of the former human self is not altogether lost. You will not lose him utterly. But he will be controlled by Molotov. Molotov will speak to his blood, control his every movement. And I don't know if even you, my dearest, will be able to get past that control. Molotov is a powerful maker; he keeps a tight leash on his progeny."

"Then..." Kalina's lips were wobbling. "Then he really is gone."

"There will be hope for him," said Octavius. "Stuart will be able to help him through it. He went through the same thing himself. And ultimately he was able to overcome his desires, even while a vampire. Stuart cares for your brother, and your brother for him. He will ease your brother's path into the underworld. He will smooth out the ways for him..." Octavius sighed. "When the Consortium was alive, it was Stuart who helped the new recruits. Spoke with them. Heard them confess to him what atrocities they had committed. At last helped them overcome their urges."

Kalina couldn't help but beam with pride when she heard this. How brave Stuart was – how strong! Now, more than ever, she was able to understand and respect what he had gone through. His struggle was her struggle. His pain was her pain. She too understood the dark and quickening nature of desire.

"He was a great vampire," she said softly. "And now he is a great man."

Octavius turned his face from her, but Kalina could see how transparent his envy was spreading across his face. They were connected now – he could hide nothing from her. His nobility was compromised by this fusing of their blood – she knew how he really felt, now. And although he was happy for Stuart, his jealousy knew no bounds.

"But you wish it had been you, don't you?" Kalina asked. "The one I turned human. Instead of Stuart."

"Let's not speak of it," Octavius waved away her concerns. "It is no matter. Stuart deserved his humanity the most. He wanted it the most."

"Not you?"

"That was never an option," Octavius said stiffly. Then he stopped, bringing them to land on a ridge of the mountain, his feet sinking into the soft snow. "Listen to me, Kalina – don't make this harder for me than it has to be. Of course I wanted you to choose me! I want it still! Why must you torment me this way, knowing I cannot..." He broke off, his savage rage quelling. "I am sorry, Kalina. I did not mean to speak so plainly. But with my blood in you, looking at your beautiful face and knowing it is my blood that runs through those veins – I cannot bring myself to do anything but love you more. I can't control it. No matter how hard I try."

Kalina stepped forward decisively and took his face in her hands, kissing him roughly. "Then don't control it," she said. "I wanted to choose you. I *chose* you. You didn't choose me. We've suffered so much, Octavius. Isn't it time?"

He rubbed her back, enveloping her in his arms. He breathed deep into her soft, perfumed hair. "I have lived thousands of years without giving in," he said. "Now I want this day with you, Kalina. To comfort you. To comfort myself. Let us give ourselves one day – one day to pretend that we could be happy together. One day to give in..." He bit his lip, biting back his desires. "I can't stand wanting you so much."

She nodded.

"This time," he said. "I will listen to my heart."

"Where are we going?" Kalina jumped on his back once more as they set flight.

"I know a place near here – far more convenient than a cave or a glade – where we can be alone." His body was trembling; he knew as well as she did what they had in mind. They flew onwards, north of the mountains, past the snowfall, until they were flying over a lush dark green forest. They flew down alongside a river, coming to rest before a once-beautiful castle, a slightly decrepit yet still-elegant fairy-tale creation that still maintained shades of its former grandeur.

"Where is this?" Kalina stepped towards the gate.

"We're in the Rhineland," said Octavius. "This castle used to belong to a friend of mine, the Baron von Blacken. He is dead now. Staked by an Armenian general in the eighteenth century. But he left the Consortium this castle in his will."

"It's beautiful," said Kalina.

"It is a place to rest," said Octavius.

They entered, their footsteps echoing throughout the empty corridors and wide chambers. There must be servants about, Kalina thought – after all, a place like this required considerable upkeep, and a fire burning in the Great Hall was a testament to some sort of occupation – but they kept their distance. Out of discretion, Kalina thought. Then, with more jealousy – did he bring all his women here?

"Come, my love." Octavius took her hand and led her upstairs. "The bedroom is this way."

Chapter 9

Octavius led Kalina up the grand marble stairs. Halfway up the stairs, he picked her up – as lightly, Kalina thought, as if she were but a feather. "We're going to do this properly," he growled, kissing her on the forehead. She loved feeling his arms around her; she nuzzled into him as he carried her up to the bedroom.

The room was the most exquisite place she'd ever seen. Silk sheets lined a canopied bed with intricately carved mahogany posts. Medieval tapestries lined the walls, and light poured into the room via a stained glass window with a Gothic point in the corner. Renaissance wardrobes, ornately designed and carved, lined one of the walls; Persian and Turkish carpets covered the floor. A roaring fire heated the room.

"For a princess," Octavius whispered. "For *my* princess." He laid her down gently on the bed. Kalina could feel the blue silk – so exquisitely soft – caressing her skin. She closed her eyes and let his mouth find its object. He kissed her gently at first, his lips lightly touching her forehead, her eyelids, her cheeks, her nose. When his mouth found hers the kiss grew rougher, more passionate. His mouth grew hungry; her hunger responded to his. She wrapped her arms around his neck, pulling him to her. She moaned softly as he nipped at her lower lips; she sighed as he swiftly removed her dressing gown.

"You must have been so cold," he whispered. "Wearing nothing but this all night." But now she was wearing nothing but lingerie, letting his mouth trace the contours of her bra and panties. She shivered with delight mingled with trepidation.

"Octavius..." she began. "I have to tell you something."

"What is it?"

"I've never done this before."

He looked up in confusion. "But Stuart..."

"No," she said, shaking her head. "It wasn't like that with him. I couldn't. I mean – I could, but I couldn't bring myself to... It wasn't that I didn't want to. I can't explain it. It didn't feel right. Octavius, it feels right now." He was kissing her neck, his mouth hot upon her cool skin. She leaned back and arched her spine as his tongue found its way to the rounded cup of her breasts. "You smell so good," he moaned. "Still, even after Molotov drained you, you manage to smell so enticing. It's driving me mad. You're regenerating, my love, I can smell it. Your Life's Blood is returning to you, driving out my blood and replacing it with your own. Normal humans – they cannot regenerate – but you..." He kissed her veins, running his tongue up and down the blue snakelike lines. Kalina shuddered with pleasure. "You are the rarest of all Carriers, Kalina," he whispered. "You're so beautiful, so special – there is nobody like you in the world. Nor has there been anyone I have met like you. Not in two thousand years."

Kalina was trembling as she felt her body react to his lips, his touch. She wanted him so badly; she could think of nothing but her desire.

"Then have me, Octavius." She sat up and stared at him. His dark eyes looked into hers, piercing her with their intense gaze. "Have me – right here, right now. If you can't turn human, Octavius, then I want you to turn me. Justin won't have to go through it alone. Please. If you turn me, I'll be immortal – I'll be safe. I have these vampire abilities now, with my blood, but it's not enough. You know it isn't enough, Octavius. I can't stand being afraid any longer. Being weak. Being vulnerable. I've already lost Justin. I can't stand to lose Stuart too..."

At the mention of Stuart's name, Kalina saw Octavius flinch.

"I couldn't help Justin, Octavius," Kalina said. "When I went into the restaurant with Stuart, I sensed something was wrong. But I didn't know what. If I'd been a vampire, I would have known. Would have sensed that it was Molotov's presence. I would have been able to do something, to stop it from happening..." Her voice quivered. "To stop Molotov from killing my brother. My Life's Blood got in the way – made me weak with desire, made me go off with Stuart."

And yet as Kalina spoke, her fierce desire gave way instead to intense sadness. *Killing my brother*, she had said. And it was true. Justin was dead –

gone. The pain echoed through her, and all the caresses and sweet kisses in the world could not hide his absence. She felt it as she would feel a knife-wound.

"Oh, my Kalina," murmured Octavius, drawing her close. He nuzzled her hair. "My love, my darling, my angel..."

"Please," said Kalina. "What do I have to stay human for? Nobody needs me to be human now. Justin was the only one. My link to the real world, the human world. To being just an ordinary Calloway from Rutherford, California – to being anyone but this Carrier. This mythical creature. And I let him die, Octavius! And he died for me. Not a vampire, not any supernatural creature – just a human being trying to do the right thing. And now he's destined to suffer a fate worse than death – and I can't even hope that my blood will be able to save him. I can't turn him back!"

"My darling..."

She sobbed into Octavius' shoulder, the full force of Justin's death hitting her at last. "Molotov will control him now..." Tears fell fast and freely. "Please, turn me. Turn me!"

"You know I can't."

"You *won't*."

"I won't."

He brushed the hair out of her face.

"Then make me forget," she said. Her voice shook. "Use compulsion – make the pain stop. Make me forget I ever had a brother – it would be better than this. Anything would be better than this."

He stroked her softly. "No, my love. I won't do that, either. Your love for Justin will live beyond him – do not act so rashly. Believe me, I want nothing in the world more than to spare you pain. But I cannot do what you ask. I love you too much to turn you – or to make you forget. These are easy ways out – but they are paths to darkness."

"But if he turns – Justin, I mean...we'll have to stake him," Kalina sobbed harder. "And Octavius, I don't think I can..."

"I'll never make you do that," said Octavius. "It will not fall to you to make that choice, that *impossible* choice. I promise you that."

Kalina looked up at him with wide eyes. "Then *you* will?"

"I will do whatever I have to do to keep you safe. And I won't let you have Justin's blood on your hands."

"It's already there," Kalina whispered. "Oh, Octavius – don't you see? It's already there!"

She sobbed herself to sleep, and as the sun crested over the castle ramparts, marking high noon, she at last fell into drowsy, exhausted oblivion. Octavius watched her sleep, stroking her hair and pressing his lips to her forehead. Letting her cry it all out. It was better that she slept, he reasoned – better that she did not feel this pain. She would have to feel it all the more keenly when she woke. Yes, Octavius knew – he would have to kill Justin as soon as he woke up. It was the only way to save him. Every moment that Justin spent alive and conscious as a vampire was a moment during which Justin would suffer unimaginable torment. Better to stake Justin just as he awakened to this new life, preventing him from ever truly understanding what a vile beast he had become.

Blood Legacy: Pulse 6

Octavius stood, tucking Kalina gently into bed. How beautiful she was, he thought, her half-naked body sparkling as the light of the early afternoon streamed through the stained glass window. Her cool, pale skin made all the whiter by her black lingerie. He wanted to press his lips to the neatly embroidered lace. But he let her sleep. Better to stifle his own desires, he knew, than to wake her and force her to contend with her loss anew.

Octavius went to the adjacent room, filling an enormous marble bathtub with hot water. His muscles ached just looking at the tub, which took up half the room, standing on gold-plated claw-feet. It had been days since he was able to take a hot bath – he had spent so long in the Alps, growing sweaty and tired as they searched in vain for the Carriers. His contacts in St. Petersburg had told him that Olga had been spotted around here, but more he did not know. He was beginning to despair. Their food and water would begin to run out soon – they were running out of time.

He removed his dressing gown and sank his muscular frame into the water, feeling its warmth against his skin, imagining it was not water at all but a lithe female frame. *Her* frame.

He had felt her pain the moment Molotov showed up at the inn. He had known immediately that things were too dangerous, that he needed to get there in the space a human heartbeat – to save her. But he had failed her. He had not come in time. He had been a fool to send her so far away – he should have kept her and Stuart near, under his protection. He had protected his own heart – so sure he would not be able to see Kalina under his roof, married to Stuart – but at what price? Had he been less selfish, he wondered grimly, had he kept Kalina with him, succumbed to the pain of wanting her, then would Justin still be alive?

At least he had saved Kalina. He could be glad of that. He knew her blood was valuable, but he wouldn't put it past Molotov to kill her all the same, sacrificing money for honor: Kalina had been instrumental in destroying Molotov's Mongolian stronghold, and Molotov knew that it was almost as important to execute her as it was profitable to keep her alive. She had destabilized the region – bringing hope to the hopeless, a chance at life for all the humans kept in Molotov's brutal "farms" for feeding.

Octavius closed his eyes, letting the sensation of the hot water wash over him. Of course, Molotov would come back once he had recovered. He would try to harm Kalina again. And Stuart, being human, was not sufficient company to protect her. He would have to be close by her at all times – fighting against his desire and love for her every step of the way. But how, he wondered, could he bear it?

Chapter 10

Octavius couldn't take his mind off her. As he soaped himself down, scrubbing the sweat from his skin, he imagined that she was there with him. Even being this far from her – she was only in the other room – was torture. He needed her, needed her with a craving stronger even than his craving for blood. How beautiful she was – how unique. Like a rare gem: the only one in the world. But she wasn't safe, he knew. Such a rare gemstone as she had to be protected. Even now, she was not safe. She had turned Stuart, but if she hadn't yet consummated her love for him, her blood would still be effective – and that meant that her blood would still send out a powerful scent to any vampires in the nearby radius looking to make a profit off her. He knew that Kalina's actions in Mongolia against Molotov had only added to her fame – vampires from Geneva to Moscow were talking about her. Who was this strange girl – who could turn vampires to human, who could fight like a vampire but sleep and eat like a human? In her, as in no Carrier before him, the true dream of the old Chinese doctor had been realized. At last, humans were able to fight back against vampires with the same abilities as vampires themselves. It had taken thousands of years, but the old doctor's legacy was finally here. She was just like a vampire in all her strengths, but had none of their weaknesses. After all, Octavius thought, Kalina had exhibited no signs of the blood-craving that caused so many vampires to go out of control.

He had not allowed himself to hope that Kalina would go back on her choice – he had resigned himself to living without her, to letting her go off with Stuart. He had dismissed any stirrings in his heart as misguided hope, a barrier against despair. But now he knew, as he sank deeper into the water, that he had always known it deep down: Kalina would never have been happy settling into a normal life, going to college, getting married young. She was destined for so much more. She was brilliant – beautiful – charismatic – she had so much to look forward to in her human life. But Kalina was so much more than just human. Her destiny was great, he knew. But would her destiny be linked with his?

Octavius stirred in surprise as he felt a hand upon his back, scrubbing his calloused flesh with a washcloth. It was a calming sensation – one to which he had grown accustomed. The servants here were trained for their discretion and for their skill in the sensual arts – the vampires who came through here needed *all* their desires satisfied.

But he didn't need a servant to satisfy his cravings this time. Not with Kalina in the next room. Thinking of her, he could not bring himself to even think about wanting anybody else. The old forms of sensuality – being pampered with massages or kisses, lithe young hands twisting and pounding into his aching muscles – no longer appealed to him. He did not want to lie back and receive the subservient pleasures a servant could offer. No, he wanted Kalina and only Kalina. Her touch was the only one that could satisfy him.

Blood Legacy: Pulse 6

And then he heard a splash, and felt the water move all about him. Somebody else had joined him in the bath.

He looked up in surprise. Kalina was sitting before him, the lapping of the water just covering her naked breasts.

"Kalina!" Her proximity was enough to drive him mad. "What are you doing here?"

"I came to take a bath..." She smiled softly. "I woke up and wanted to warm up...the bed was so cold...and then I found you."

He could make out the contours of her form beneath the waters of the bath. She leaned in to kiss him, moaning softly as his lips parted beneath hers. "We didn't finish what we came for," she said, pushing her palms against his broad chest, pushing him back against the marble bathtub. Her eyes were wide with playful mock-innocence.

Octavius gave a deep sigh. How could he resist her – especially when she was so close to him? He could smell her, breathing in her intoxicating scent, her blood driving him mad, driving him to distraction. How could any man resist a woman like her? How could any vampire? She was sensuality personified – the Life's Blood creating in her a sensuality that drove him mad.

"You know exactly how to make me weak at the knees," he murmured, bringing her naked frame closer to him. "You know exactly what to do."

She kissed him, placing his hand upon her breasts. "Have you thought some more about what I asked?" Kalina looked up at him innocently. "Have you considered changing your mind?"

So that was what she wanted. He saw steel in her eyes – Kalina wanted to be turned, and she was going to do whatever it took to get what she wanted. How cunning she was – how clever! A woman like that was not to be taken lightly. But how he wanted to take her!

She took the soap and began lathering him up, pressing her lithe fingers into his back.

"Well, have you?" She leaned in and kissed his ear.

"No," he said hoarsely. "I won't turn you." His voice was grim. "No, there is no way I could do that, Kalina."

Blood Legacy: Pulse 6

"Why not?"

"Because," Octavius sighed. This was the hardest thing he'd ever had to do. "You have a gift. A destiny. You can't just give that up. No matter how much you love me, Kalina. No matter how much I love you – you have a destiny that goes beyond our love. That brings you further from me than I can bear. But I cannot bring myself to take that destiny from you."

Kalina rose from the water, the soap clinging to her white, milky flesh. She was like Venus rising from the foam before him – the most beautiful thing he'd ever seen. He had seen the most beautiful maidens in the world in his day, but none of them ever compared with her. Octavius stared up at her, stunned. Her beauty was overwhelming – indeed, it seemed that she had never been so beautiful as she was at this moment. She was regenerating, he knew. Her Life's Blood was returning to her, stronger than ever, making her more beautiful and more powerful than she had been ever before. And that meant, he knew, that her Life's Blood was slowly taking over from his blood in her. Soon their close bond would reset – the glory of the past few hours gone. Octavius sighed. It would happen sooner or later, he knew – their connection would go back to what it had been before. She would still love him, but they wouldn't have this same electric connection – a connection that made it impossible for him to resist her, and for her to resist him. He would have to compete once more with Jaegar and Stuart for her attention. And she wouldn't be able to see into his soul the way she did when his blood was in her body. She wouldn't be able to tell how much he loved her; she wouldn't be able to see the longing and desire in his eyes. He would have to push her away again. He knew that they couldn't remain like this – this weakened by their dual desire – forever. He knew that things would have to go back to normal – he would have to feign distance in order to protect her. And she would no longer be able to see through his mental defenses. She would no longer understand how much he loved her.

She saw the best in him – the side he didn't show to anyone else. To the others he had to be brave and strong, honorable and without emotion.

Blood Legacy: Pulse 6

He had to set an example for the other vampires – to behave better than the best of them, to inspire them to greatness. But behind closed doors, he could be soft. He could be tender. He could give himself over to love. She saw the humanity in him – a humanity he could not bear to lose.

Oh, why did he not turn her? Octavius raged against his sense of duty. How he longed to have his blood in her forever, to turn her into a vampire, to have her at his side all through what he knew would be an agonizing eternity of loneliness. If he turned her, he knew, she would have his blood in her for always; her Life's Blood would stop regenerating to wash away his influence on her. How happy he would be, he thought – an eternity with the woman he loved beyond reason.

But he loved her too much to let her do that. He loved her too much to destroy her life.

And the sun was falling in the sky. They would have to go back. They would have to face the truth.

He rose from the water, his chest glistening with soap. He went over to her, taking her hands, looking deep into her eyes, her nakedness rosy in the glimmer of sunset.

I love you so much, Kalina. Please do not be angry with me for my choice.

Her face fell.

"I love you too," said Kalina sadly. "I just wish it could always be like this."

"Believe me, Kalina, so do I."

He bent over to kiss her, then, running his fingers through her sweet, perfumed wet hair. A kiss full of promise – and fuller still of regret.

Chapter 11

At last they broke apart, Octavius running his hands up and down her naked body. "You should get dressed," he said softly. "As much as I enjoy seeing you like this – it's almost time to go. And it's cold out – colder still by nightfall. We need to get back soon. I have collected clothing here over the years – some may well be your size. Your dressing-gown was covered in blood..."

"Other clothes?" Kalina looked down. Had Octavius brought other women here over the years?

But she did not resist as she picked out a fur-lined jacket and wool pants, supplementing the outfit with warm gloves, a scarf, and leather boots. This was going to be a difficult night for her, she knew, and she couldn't risk making herself sick. She would have to watch Justin turn – and she had no idea what she would do next. Thinking about Justin was making her crazy. How could she even bring herself to imagine what he would go through the moment he opened his eyes, the moment he realized that something was wrong?

"Justin..." Kalina sighed heavily. "It's time to go back. We have to see him." She wiped away the tears budding at the corners of her eyelids. "No matter what. I'm his little sister," her voice trembled. "It's my job to be there for him, no matter what." She leaned in to embrace Octavius one last time, pressing the fur of her coat against his bare skin. Even without direct contact, touching him filled her with wanting. "I want to thank you," she said. "For being there for me. For being there when I needed you. I don't know what I would have done if I'd spent the day waiting – alone in the room, with Justin, with his body..."

Her voice began to shake.

Octavius nodded solemnly, taking her hands in his. "I understand completely," he said, stroking Kalina's hair. "You know, my dearest Kalina, that there is nothing I wouldn't do for you. You know how much I would do for you – how much I will *always* do for you. I love you, and nothing will change that, no matter what happens." He led her downstairs via the Grand Staircase. "I know you love history," he said. "Its art. Its culture. Its treasures." He smiled sadly. "If only we had more time here – I could show you all around. Tell you about these rooms. Give you their history. Tell you stories. Show you artifacts." He sighed. "Perhaps one day we will come here again." It was an impossible dream, Kalina knew. This was a one-day thing – a result of her grief and the pumping of his blood in her veins. Once the Life's Blood in her regenerated, once the immediacy and numbness of her grief subsided, things would go back to normal. They would never have a day like this together again.

This time the journey back was quicker, and the sun was still golden in the air by the time they arrived back at the inn. "It's much faster," Kalina noted. "I thought we were much further off," she mused.

"I must confess to a bit of deceit," Octavius said. "I took you intentionally by the longer route. I wanted to spend as much time as possible alone with you – I didn't want to be without you for a single second." He smiled, his white teeth glimmering in the pink of sunset. "It felt so good, having you wrap your thighs around my chest, your arms around my neck. A pleasant weight." He held her tighter. "Woman, you are torture to be around when one can't have you."

Kalina laughed. It felt good to laugh again, the midst of so much pain. "Maybe one time we can take that long route again," she said.

He sighed. "I would like that very much." He squeezed her hand as they flew faster. "One day," he said.

"One day."

What a happy dream, Kalina thought – and what an impossible reality. Too much divided them, she knew. But their love was stronger than ever.

"Too late this time, though." Octavius nodded as the inn came into view before them. And then they were back in Kalina's room, Justin lying pale and pallid upon the bed. She had always known that it was coming, that Justin's body was there, but as she looked at him somehow Kalina felt that it was still a shock to her. Her whole body recoiled in horror; her blood burned her veins. This wasn't a dream. This was real. Her brother was lying dead before her.

Suddenly, all her thoughts of Octavius, of their snowy moonlight journey, of their fairy-tale day together in the castle, simply vanished. They were like a dream from which she had just awakened; she had returned into the harsh cruelty of truth.

Max and Stuart were standing vigil over Justin, watching him closely for any signs of turning. Max's face was grim and angry; Stuart's eyes were wide with pain, all the blood drained from his face.

They looked up at Kalina and Octavius as they entered, and Stuart's eyes lit up with relief. "Kalina!" he cried, running to embrace her. His strong arms encircled her slender shoulders. "We didn't know what happened to you – we thought you were injured. Your moth...I mean, Max, said that you were still alive, that she'd have felt it if you were dead, but we weren't sure."

Max said nothing, but only stared blankly at Kalina.

"Where were you?" Stuart examined her for any signs of injury, his hands running up and down her body. "We were so worried about you! Molotov took so much out of you..." His eyes fell upon her neck, where two puncture wounds had been replaced by clean, new skin. "How did you..." He looked up at Octavius and there he found his answer. "He healed you."

"I did," said Octavius warily.

Stuart tried to mask the savage jealousy that came over his face, but he could not. Kalina could hear straight through into his heart, his deepest and innermost thoughts. *I never thought I would wish myself a vampire again. But now it is what I wish. It should have been my blood that healed her – not his. It is I who have bonded with her, and not he! Not my former maker, who condemned me to so many centuries of torment! If anyone should have saved her...*

Kalina's eyes widened with shock. She nearly fell over in surprise. Stuart had spent seven hundred years of his vampire life hating every minute of it. Would he really be willing to go through all that immortal torture again? For her? *I have tasted her blood. I know its fruits. She had called out to me twice. She is mine now. I won't let Octavius have her, not if it kills me. He is no longer my maker; I owe him no blood loyalty. I will fight him if I must. I will stake him, if only it means...*

"Stuart!" Kalina interrupted his thoughts, taking his hands in hers. "You watched Justin for me. I can't thank you enough..." Her voice was soft and soothing, and Stuart looked at least temporarily mollified. "I could never do this without you."

Stuart's hurt and anger seemed to subside; his expression took on a new gentleness. He wrapped his arms around her, stroking her hair. Octavius looked almost angry as Stuart kissed Kalina's forehead. "I'm so sorry, Kalina," he said. "I'm sorry I wasn't able to save him in time. I too know what it is like to lose a brother. And Justin was like a brother to me."

Kal hugged him back, her mind shuffling through memories of him. She remembered the first time they had embraced, when she had comforted him over what she thought was Aaron's death. Stuart knew the depths of her pain, as only someone who had lost a sibling could understand. Immediately as they touched, she felt a familiar heat in her skin. The familiar sign that Octavius' influence was wearing off – her Life's Blood was reacting with Stuart's blood again. With each new pint of blood that her body brought forth, her connection with Stuart would grow stronger, her connection with Octavius weakening.

She looked up apologetically at Octavius, but his expression was a cipher to her. Only hours before, she had felt as if she were able to see into his very soul. But now she felt no such thing. He was as distant from her as he had always been. Kalina's heart ached with his loss – even as her body responded to Stuart's touch.

Poor Stuart. He had always been so kind to her, so good. From the start, he had loved her; he had treated her so wonderfully! Always made her feel special. Needed. Loved.

And Justin had loved him too. Kalina felt tears come to her eyes as she remembered how Stuart had made breakfast for her and Justin, how the two of them had bonded. Justin had always wanted her to choose Stuart – always secretly hoped that the two of them would end up brothers. Two nice guys used to doing things for the women they loved. And now

Blood Legacy: Pulse 6

Justin was dead, and Stuart was heartbroken and alone. Had she let Justin down, she wondered? In more ways than one, Kalina knew, as she walked over to Justin's body, taking his cold hand in hers.

Stuart knelt down alongside him, pressing his face into his hands, which were clasped at his front.

"What are you doing?" Kalina turned to him.

He took Justin's other hand. "I have been praying for him," he said solemnly. "After Octavius went after you, I stayed here with Justin. I prayed for him. I left for a while – Max took over the vigil – and I went into town until I found a church a few miles from here, a wonderful Medieval church with stained glass windows. A church from my old time. And do you know – it was the first time since turning human that I felt a truly religious experience? I spent hours kneeling on the cold marble, my face pressed to the floor. Praying for your brother." He sighed heavily. "I only wish that God would grant me my prayers."

Chapter 12

The night wore on. The waiting was the worst part. At least when she was far off in the Rhineland with Octavius, she could forget. Now there was no forgetting. There was only staying and watching. Kalina's eyelids grew heavy more than once as she sat in the chair, sleep proving a more merciful mistress than wakefulness. She drowsily noted at one point that she was in Stuart's arms, that he was carrying her to the adjacent room, whispering to her comforting tales to calm her. Stories of his childhood in England, of a boyhood spent idolizing the great Knights Templar of that era, of how he longed to be at once a soldier and a man of God as they were. She only half-heard them, so close was she to complete slumber, but as she drifted into sleep proper she found that she was dreaming of the world of which Stuart spoke. She dreamed of two boys, each one handsomer than the other, young and strong and full of vigor, playing at swords and daggers. Two boys – one soft and kind, the other passionate and cocksure. Stuart and Jaegar – the brothers – clad in simple tunics and leather belts.

Yet her dream took her beyond their childhood. She dreamed of Stuart and Jaegar growing up. Being turned. And then Stuart faded from her dream, and Jaegar took center stage. Suddenly she was in a dark room, alone with Jaegar. He was no longer in Medieval garb; his clothing was tight yet tailored, perfectly modern. A stylish black silk shirt, black slacks. The outfit he had worn on the day she first met him. He was more beautiful than she remembered him, his face perfect in every way. His blue eyes blazing, looking at her with a mixture of adoration and desire. But she sensed there was danger in him, too. Some lurking need, some uncontrollable longing, bubbling just beneath the surface. One wrong move – one step too far in the direction of passion – and he would snap. Seize her. Take her. She didn't remember him being this beautiful. But he took a step towards her, and lightly stroked her bared shoulders.

How strange! She was dreaming – and yet Jaegar's touch felt so vivid. So real. "Kalina," he whispered, and his voice sounded real too, "I had to see you. I had to talk to you. I'm sorry it's been so long…"

This was no dream, Kalina knew. Whatever she was seeing before her was no figment of her imagination, but the real Jaegar. Her Life's Blood was beginning to prickle and burn just as it always did when Jaegar was around.

"What are you doing here?" Kalina heard herself say. "Like this – in my dreams? What's going on?"

Jaegar stepped forward, taking her hands in his. "Because I know you need me," said Jaegar. "I told myself I'd keep away, but when I sensed what happened to Justin, I knew you needed somebody else to come and comfort you. Believe me, Kalina, I too mourn for Justin. The moment I felt him die, well, it was like losing Aaron again." He shuddered "I had to come and see you. I don't want to disturb your peace – I have done my best to wish you and Stuart every happiness in the world. I don't want to intrude upon that now. But I am ready to come to you as a friend, if you need me. To me, of course, you will always be so much more, but I will take whatever it is you grant me." His eyes were haunted, so full of sadness. "I missed you, Kal." He gathered her into his arms, folding her tightly into his chest.

"But how are you here?" Kalina looked up into his face, feeling him smolder beneath that look of quiet intensity. "What's going on? What are you doing here?"

"You and I still have that bond, Kalina. We never lost it. I tried to shut it off for a while to protect you, to prevent you from seeing my pain. But now I know I cannot shut off our connection forever. I need you, just like you need me. And my powers have only grown stronger in the past few weeks. I've learned to dreamwalk, a skill only old and ancient vampires can know. Our telepathy now extends to dreams. I can enter yours. And you, if you wish, can enter mine." He pressed his lips to her forehead. "I missed you so much."

"I missed you too," Kalina confessed with a sigh. "So much. When you left us in China, when I couldn't find you – I was so afraid something had happened to you, or that you were so angry that you no longer wanted anything to do with me. Living without you has been like living with a giant hole in my heart."

"I just wanted you to know," Jaegar reached out and touched her. "That you don't have to mourn for him. Justin was like a brother to me in life – in death, too, he'll be my brother. I'll watch over him. I'll take care of him. Help him to overcome his urges. Help him to become free of the bond his maker has over him."

"But how?" Kalina was about to ask, when a loud knock on the door sent her spinning into wakefulness. She sat up with a start, Stuart too leaping to his feet. Max had rushed in, her face grim. "It's happening," she said quickly. "He's waking up. Hurry!"

Kalina and Stuart leaped out of bed and rushed down the hall. There he was, just as Max had said. Justin was sitting straight up. Kalina gasped when she saw him. His skin was paler, as pale as death, with a haggard look at once beautiful and awful. His slender body had grown broader, stronger; his skin had smoothed over the first early signs of aging. The dark circles under his eyes – an occupational hazard of the medical profession – had vanished. Kalina didn't even have to check his fangs. She knew, with a horrible sinking feeling, that Justin had turned. The Justin who sat before her was a vampire.

"Kal?" Justin's eyes widened when Kalina entered. "What's going on? I don't feel so good..." He put out a hand to steady himself on the bed. "But then again – I feel *really* good. I don't understand..." He immediately jumped to his feet. Kal took an instinctive step back; Stuart stepped in between her and Justin, his stance protective.

"Tell me how you feel," Octavius said softly. "Go on, Justin."

"Did I get hit in the head?" Justin's hands flew to his temple. "I feel like I was hit with a brick. My head is throbbing. Like...I hear something. This loud beating sound. Like the world's loudest clock – tock, tock, tock. No, it's not a clock at all. It's like what you hear on a stethoscope...but louder. Like a heartbeat." He looked around wildly, confused. "And what's that smell? Something sweet..." He stepped up to Stuart. "You smell so good..." He looked Stuart up and down.

And then it happened. His fangs flew from his lips, following quickly by a short, sharp yelp of surprise. And pain.

"Justin!" Kalina cried.

"Oh, no." Justin's eyes flew open even wider. "Oh, no, no, no, no, no...." His fingers went to his mouth, and he felt the two decisive prongs of fangs at the corners of his lips. "No...it can't be." He looked up at Octavius in horror. "Did *you* do this?" His voice exploded in rage.

Octavius shook his head mutely.

"Then I don't understand..."

Kalina stepped forward, putting a hand on her brother's shoulder. "Molotov attacked you," she said. "But first he drank from himself and then made you drink...he wanted to punish you, punish all of us..."

"Molotov...turned me?" Justin looked so innocent, so pained. How could she bear to tell him the news?

"Yes." It was the hardest thing she'd ever had to say.

"Then *he's* my maker? He controls me?" Justin's eyes began to water with bloody tears. "No, he can't! He won't! I won't let him!"

"Listen, Justin," Stuart said calmly. "Don't panic. We know what you've been through –we've all been there. We'll help you. We'll do what we can when you need us to help break Molotov's bond with you. We brought vampire wine..."

"You should have just staked me when you had the chance," Justin moaned. "How could you keep me alive like this – a danger to everybody? A danger to my own sister?"

Octavius looked grimly at Kalina. Almost, she wondered, as if he agreed.

"Listen, if I do anything dangerous...you need to stake me."

And then she saw the stake in Octavius' hand. "I'm sorry, Justin," he said. "I can't afford to wait that long!"

"No!" Kalina cried, rushing forth to stop the blow Octavius was about to strike. The wood collided with her hand, bruising her. A small amount of blood appeared from a splinter-wound.

And then Justin was sniffing the air, leaping upon her like a wild beast, his fangs making their way to her hand.

"Don't!" Immediately Max and Stuart were holding him back.

"No..." Justin was moaning. "No – I want it. I need it!" Bloody tears streaked his cheeks. "But I can't....I can't do this. I want her...but you can't let me hurt her! Just stake me now! Go on, Octavius, do it! If you do it before I've killed somebody, at least I have a chance..."

"You'll be able to control it," said Stuart. "Vampire wine."

"I don't *want* your damned wine!" Justin roared, in a voice that was not Justin's at all, but the tone of a stranger. "I want *her*!" The expression on his face was hard and cruel – a voice Kalina did not recognize. It sent chills down her spine. "I want to hurt her...kill her..." Then Justin's face relaxed – he was his old self again, shaking with terror. "Stop me," he said in a small voice. "This *thing* inside of me, it's taking over, it wants me. This voice in my head, Molotov's voice, commanding me to kill her...make it stop!"

"Molotov's already waiting to use him against us," said Octavius gravely. "I should have known."

"You fools!" Justin was roaring, opening his mouth wide and revealing his ever-growing fangs. "I want to kill – I will kill. Give me the girl! I want to suck her, to drain her dry, to make her..."

"Justin, stop!" Kalina screamed. "Listen to me – it's me! It's Kalina!"

"I...can't..." once more it was the real Justin, the Justin she loved, her brother, trying to keep control as his whole body shook.

"Molotov's too strong," said Octavius darkly. "He'll never be able to resist. It's too dangerous letting him live. He's willing to die, Kalina – we cannot let him live like this. This *vampire* is not your brother."

"Please, don't!"

But Justin had broken free of Stuart and Max's grasp, and had rushed over to Kalina.

"I must do it now." Octavius raised his stake, glimmering with the red light of its rubies. "I'm sorry, Kalina."

"*No!*"

But it was not Kalina who pushed Justin out of the way, but Max. Her former silence gave way to a quiet intensity, like the slow smoldering of a coal flame. "Go," she whispered to Justin, putting herself between him and Octavius. "Run!" Justin looked at her in bewilderment as Max picked him up, her strong arms easily overpowering the newly-turned vampire, and threw him out the window.

They rushed to the window, watching Justin fall as Kalina had fell, only to watch his body break the fall with instinctive flight.

"Go!" Max called. "Run!"

And then Justin was gone – vanished into the night sky.

Kalina was still shaking. She turned to Octavius, hurt and anger across her face. "How could you do that?" Her voice trembled. "Octavius, that was *Justin.*"

Blood Legacy: Pulse 6

"No," said Octavius, shaking his head. "That wasn't Justin at all. I'm sorry, Kalina – but Molotov controls him now. He's no less dangerous than Molotov himself. He is programmed to go after you until one of you is killed. And while I do sympathize for your care for your brother, it is not you that I will let die before my eyes."

"But you saved him," Kalina turned to her mother, feeling weak and dizzy. She sat down as the room became blurry all around us.

"I have some Life's Blood in Justin yet," said Max. "From last time, when I saved him. While it has grown weaker as a result of Molotov's influence, it is there nonetheless. And Justin will go to Molotov now. He will help to lead us there."

"We don't want to go *to* Molotov!" Kalina cried. "We want to get as far away from that crazy...bastard as we can."

"Then how do you expect to break Molotov's hold over your brother?" snapped Max. "Nothing is impossible in the world of the vampire, Kalina. Not even that. But without Molotov, we cannot break the bond. If we slay Molotov, Justin will still be a vampire, but at least he will be a vampire in control of himself. He will drink vampire wine. Stuart and I will work with him. Right now he is a danger, to himself as well as to you. And to save him, we must go into danger ourselves."

Chapter 13

Max's expression softened. She went over to Kalina, wrapping her spindly arms around Kalina's slender dark shoulders. "Listen, my girl," she said. "Don't panic. Justin isn't dead – if anything, he has a whole eternity in which to be saved. We can't turn him back – neither one of us can love him in the way that love needs to operate to turn him – but we may be able to find another Carrier who can. Or even if he is a vampire, all is not lost. Look at Jaegar and Octavius – they were able to find happy enough lives as vampires."

Kalina looked up mournfully. She knew that, for all their pretended strength, neither Jaegar nor Octavius was really happy as a vampire. Max stroked Kalina's hair. "Listen, I'll be able to track Justin now. If he still has my Life's Blood in me, it makes him special. It means he'll have a better time tracking down the Carriers Mal hid – and I don't doubt

Molotov is aware of the fact. He's probably using Justin right now to trace the Carriers. If we follow Justin's trail, we may be able to find both him and the Carriers."

"You saved his life," Kalina was still trying to process everything, to put everything together. "You did that for him!"

"He is family," said Max. "Your family – and so he is my family. He has my blood in him – I could not forget that. I have hope for him. These are confusing times for Carriers, Kalina. We do not know what the blood will do, what powers it will bring forth. Your blood is special; the blood of the younger Carriers may prove to be more special still. How can we give up hope when this blood may help us win the fight we have been waging for centuries?"

"You said the love would only work if it were...you, know. Romantic."

"I believe so," said Max. "After all, the links between blood and sex are strong with vampires – the one and the other cannot be separated. Your love for your brother may not be able to turn him." She smiled. "But there are more Carriers in the world than you and I, Kalina. And your brother is a good man. He will find somebody one of these days, I have confidence of that."

Octavius interrupted them, clearing his throat as he put on his leather jacket, arranging his stakes in a belt around his waist. "Kalina," he said softly. "I must go now. I believe I have a plan..."

"You're not going after Justin, are you?" Kalina's eyes widened in fear. "Octavius, please say you're not. Max thinks he could turn back – her Life's Blood in him might be able to help him stay strong."

"I'll see you again, Kalina," Octavius said, evading the question. "I promise you that."

She wrapped her arms around him. "But where are you going?" She asked.

"When I was the leader of the Consortium my duties were to find more Carriers. To match them to worthy vampires. To help arrange love-matches – love I could not participate in myself. I know how to sense out these things. I will go to Africa, to Australia, to continents we have not yet been to; I will seek out a Carrier who is willing to meet with your brother, perhaps to fall in love with him."

Kalina was speechless. She knew that Octavius' instincts were to stake Justin as quickly as possible – nevertheless, he was willing to do as she wished.

"You might not need to go that far," said Max. "I felt something earlier today – there's the smell of Life's Blood in the air here. Don't go too quickly." She too began dressing, putting on her warmest furs. "I'll show you where," she said to Octavius.

"You're the boss," Octavius bowed deeply to Max, giving Kalina a little sly wink as he did so. Kalina couldn't help but smile. Even now, Octavius was trying to appease her.

Max took hold of Kalina's hands. "I'll leave you with Stuart," she said. "You're in good hands here.

He told me what happened with the two of you. You made the right choice, Kalina. You didn't let your blood make that decision for you. I'm proud of you. Perhaps he is the wrong one. Or perhaps he is the right one – and you aren't ready for any right ones yet. Whatever the reason, you should wait until you find yourself ready to choose." She let a smile spread over her face. "You and I are alike, Kalina. I found myself in a similar position with your father. But in the end..."

"Things worked out?"

Max said nothing. Kalina wondered what had really happened to her father, a topic on which Max had always been so coy. But Stuart interrupted her before she could ask further.

"Where are you going?" Kalina asked, noticing Stuart's jacket.

"I'm coming with you all," said Stuart. "I know it's risky – but I'm willing to risk my life. I'd rather die a noble human than live for centuries as a vampire. I've turned – and that turning was a miracle. But with this saved and blessed human life, I want to make the most of the time I have left: I want to do something good to make up for all the bad I have done." He took Kalina's hand. "I need to find these kids – and help you do it. Or else, what's worth living for?"

Kalina smiled right back at Stuart. How noble he was – how brave! Even now he was willing to risk his very humanity in order to do the right thing. His enormous piercing eyes stared into hers, and she could see the goodness in them. Stuart was special, she knew; Stuart had something that Octavius and Jaegar lacked. A true humanity. Stuart's nobility ran through him like blood – permeating all parts of him – transforming his beautiful but all-too-human frame into something more than human. Kalina knew that Stuart wouldn't be able to fight as he was once able to; this gift that she had given him was in that sense also a curse. Kalina sighed as she pressed his hands to her lips. She tasted the warm blush of his skin, and as her lips met his knuckles she had to force herself to look back up at him before the desire to sink her teeth into his flesh overtook her. Octavius' blood was wearing off, she knew, and as Life's Blood began to pulse once more through her veins Kalina began to feel that same old attraction she had felt towards Stuart – an attraction so strong that it even compelled her to put Justin's life in danger, to leave the dining room and take Stuart up to the suite, a desire that demanded instant satisfaction for the longing she felt all through her body.

Stuart seemed to notice the change in her eyes. "What is it, my sweet?" he asked her softly. He knew, Kalina realized, he could tell how much she wanted him still. No, she told herself, it wasn't safe to remain alone with him – not for her, and not for Stuart either. If she was left alone with Stuart, she would either succumb to her desire to be with him or her desire to consume him, and neither of them would be of any help to Justin or the Carriers. Kalina swallowed down her hunger. If all this worked out, she told herself, if they survived and were able to save Justin and the Carriers, she'd need to find a cure for this savage hunger that overtook her at the slightest whiff of sweet blood. She wasn't a vampire, after all. So why was she starting to behave like one.

"Hold on, boys," Kalina said, turning to Octavius. "And Max. I don't think we should split up; it's a bad idea. We need to stick together if we want to stay safe. I can't defend Stuart on my own; now that he's only human he's in more danger than ever before." Kalina didn't mention that she feared Stuart was in just as much danger from her as he was in from vampires proper. "If you two leave to find other Carriers we'll be in danger. Let's get to Molotov first, try to break the spell. Then we can all seek out Carriers together. And maybe there will be some older Carriers among the ones in captivity – we can kill two birds with one stone."

Max and Octavius looked at each other, reconsidering their plan. Although their telepathy was weaker than it had been, Kalina could faintly make out what was going on inside Octavius' head.

But no, Kalina, my sweet Kalina, how can you put me through such torment? How can you ask me to be by your side, to tolerate proximity, when all I want to do is kiss you, and lose myself in your sweet love? I want to take you right here, right now, the others be damned...

Kalina blushed scarlet, hoping that the others didn't see the fruits of her desire spreading out across her rosy face. She felt exactly as Octavius did. But she hoped that having both Stuart and Octavius near her would counteract each of her attractions; wanting them both, she would be able to go after neither.

"Kalina has a point," concluded Max, her jaw and expression decisive. "We can't risk leaving them alone. We're strongest as a team – and as a team we should stay. I can track Justin – Kalina can make out the Carriers. And Stuart's nose was once effective at this sort of thing..."

"No longer," Stuart bowed his head.

"No, Stuart – you'll just have to try harder." Max wasn't in the mood for understanding. "Human or vampire, you know what Life's Blood smells like, and we need all the help we can get. Now, before we were side-tracked, we were making our way through the Devil's Mouth, one of the most dangerous mountain passes in the Alps. We'll need to dress warmly, to bring supplies, and to stock up on weapons. This is no easy place for humans – Stuart, you may want to hang back..."

"Not a chance," said Stuart. "If I die, I die fighting the good fight."

"Then understand," Max began, in that swift, business-like way of hers, "that if you are taken prisoner, we cannot risk our position to save you. Even if they threaten to turn you again. You come at your own risk."

Stuart turned white with fear, and Kalina felt her color draining in response. But he nodded anyway. "I understand the risks," he said. "I take them gladly. Whatever I can do to help Kalina here."

He turned his wide eyes to her, and once again Kalina began to feel overwhelmed at the enormity of Stuart's love. He was a good man, she knew – one that truly deserved her love. She knew now that he did not love her merely for her blood, as she had feared, but indeed for herself, for even though he was human he was willing to risk all that for a chance to convince her that *he*, and not Octavius or Jaegar, was the one she really loved. Was he really willing to risk everything if it meant a shot at getting her back? Kalina's eyes filled with tears, so greatly did his actions touch her.

"Thanks, Stuart," she squeezed his hand. "You're a real..."

But she stopped herself before saying *friend.* Was Stuart not more than a friend to her – after all, if Molotov hadn't come in when he had, she might have given herself to Stuart, totally and completely? She certainly felt an attraction to him. And hadn't Max said that Kalina's troubled feelings might be a result not of indecision but of her youth – maybe she just wasn't ready to settle down with Stuart, but might be one day? Had not Max done something similar with Kalina's own father?

Kalina sighed. "Never mind," she said quietly. "Let's go. We have some Carriers to save."

"Let's go!" They all echoed. "For the Carriers! For Justin!"

Chapter 14

And so they decided to set off for the Devil's Mouth. Stuart and Octavius both strained their noses, but ultimately it was Max who best knew the way. They had spent a few hours getting ready, collecting supplies from a safe-house Max and Stuart had used in the area, but now they were hot on the trail just as dawn began to illuminate their path. Octavius was slightly bristling under the sun, even though his Life's Blood ring was on his finger, keeping him safe from the true power of the rays. But he did not complain. If he was uncomfortable under the sun, even while wearing a Life's Blood ring, then other vampire guards would be equally – if not more – weakened. At daytime he had only to worry about the Life's Blood vampires – those who had drunk Carrier blood and were able to walk in the sunlight even without the rings. He knew that Kalina and he had staked most of the Life's Blood vampires back in Mongolia; the ruby stakes they all carried would take care of the rest. He doubted there would be many left of Molotov's old army; Molotov couldn't have access to more than a few Life's Blood rings, bought – he imagined – on the black market, or else stolen by Mal's men from the Consortium during the time of the great slaughter in Rome. Octavius narrowed his gaze and frowned as he remembered that terrible night, as he watched all his trusted friends and comrades, fellow-generals all, die before his very eyes. Die for Kalina's sake – and for his. They had fought well until the end, he knew. Fought bravely. But that did not make their loss any easier. He still missed them; their loss was still torture to him. The final end of his centuries of work filled his dreams with agony, and made him wake up in the middle of the day, sweating out nightmares.

The Consortium had once been a thing of greatness, Octavius knew. A group of vampires all working together, dedicated to eradicating the evil and chaos they saw in the world. Dedicating to preserving the lives and blood of Carriers. All good and true men and women, willing to sacrifice their desires for the good of the many. Men he had himself turned, condemning them to an eternity of tortuous hunger, and yet they never blamed him. They never resented him for their turning. They simply served him well.

And now they were dead – gone. Staked into nothingness – for if there was an afterlife for vampires, Octavius had never heard of it. Indeed, the vampires he knew feared death even more than humans did – perhaps their immortality destroyed in them any faith in the hereafter. It had been Mal who had staked them, but he had done so at Molotov's bidding. Molotov was behind the destruction of the Consortium – his greed had known no bounds of decency or honor. Octavius grimaced. Molotov might pretend to be an honorable, reasonable vampire – a more noble creature than the mad blood-thirsty rogues who wandered the streets at night willy-nilly, looking for victims – but really he was no better than the rest. No, Octavius thought to himself as they made their way towards the Devil's Mouth once more, this meeting with Molotov would be a personal one. This was no longer a theoretical battle – a battle for power between two evenly-matched vampires. This was a chance for revenge. To avenge the Consortium, to avenge Justin...

It was personal, now.

He carried a normal stake in his left hand, but slung over his right arm was a machine-gun cleverly outfitted to dispense flying ruby-encrusted stakes at hundreds of miles an hour. Molotov may be weakened, Octavius knew, but this time he wasn't going to take any chances. It was time for the ragged remnants of the Consortium to go high-tech; now stake-guns and sprayers dispensing powdered rubies served them just as well as the traditional stake of wood.

Because Octavius wasn't going to risk losing. The fate of the Carriers, of Justin, of whatever future the Consortium held, depended upon their victory. He was going to make Molotov pay.

Yet the absence of vampires at dawn slightly

perturbed him. If it was true that the Carriers were being kept here, surely the vampires commissioned to stand guard wouldn't have been able to resist taking a sip or two of fresh Carrier blood – and surely in that case there would be plenty of guards standing about in the morning, instead of going to ground as they seemed to have done. The eerie silence seemed to presage stillness, a false, dead end. But Max insisted that she smelled Carrier blood in the air and led them onwards.

The Devil's Mouth was a savage, terrifying place. Jagged mountainsides, like skeletons or knife-edges, rose up above them. White snow beds, untouched and yet terrifying in their whiteness, seemed to surround them on all sides, so that not five miles into their journey Kalina and the others lost all sense of direction or orientation. Everything was white; everything was mountainous; everything was snow. This place was like a labyrinth, drawing them in deeper, closing up all around them, so that even the tracks they meticulously tried to leave in the snow vanished within minutes as more avalanches and snowfall buried the footprints in new layers of snow. Kalina shuddered as she sniffed the air, picking up on the scent of Life's Blood. Had Mal really hidden *children* here? At eighteen, she still found this place daunting; it gave her the chills. But to leave children – some as young as eight or ten – in a place like that? Such cruelty astounded her.

"I can't believe it," Kalina sighed. "I always knew that Mal was evil, but even I could never imagine that he'd be this bad. Rotten, through and through." She remembered what Mal had done to her and grimaced. The tortures he had put her through still gave her nightmares. But no matter what Mal had done to her, at least she was seventeen when it had happened. Old enough to pull herself together and make it through. Kalina thought back to her childhood. As a ten-year-old, she knew, she never would have been able to find the strength to get out of there alive...

"They're just kids," Kalina said aloud, the wind of the mountains almost swallowing up her words.

Blood Legacy: Pulse 6

"I know," Stuart shuddered. "Awful, isn't it? Mal was truly...a monster. Many vampires have some good in them, however deep down, but not Mal. Who knows what he was like in life? I'd guess that even before he was turned, he was a piece of..."

Max cut in. "Even if the Carriers managed to escape," she said, "they wouldn't survive long out here. Not under conditions like this. Kids with no understanding of who they were or *what* they were, no idea how to navigate a mountain or climb...it would probably kill a Carrier, let alone a normal child."

"Unless that's why there are no guards standing out here," Octavius said. "I was wondering about that myself. Why would Mal risk the children escaping? Unless that was part of his plan..."

"What do you mean?" Kalina asked.

"Yes, it all makes sense now," Octavius nodded. "Mal wanted them to try to escape. He knew the Carriers would make it out – eventually – at least, most of them would. And that the humans would die trying. He's probably sent guards to find them eventually...but not until the humans have been killed off by the cold and the snow and the other animals out here."

The howling of a wolf in the distance punctuated this last remark.

"Then he wouldn't have to spend money and time on dealing with humans," said Kalina. "He could focus on the ones he was sure were Carriers – by letting *children* die!" She clapped a hand over her mouth. "That really is despicable."

"It also means that our job is that much harder," said Octavius. "If Carriers are out here, then they're probably spread out at this point, not left in a single place. And we can only sniff out Carriers – if there are any human girls left out here at this rate, we won't be able to identify their blood as easily. I can sniff out humans to some extent – but their blood's nowhere near as strong as Carrier blood."

Kalina felt her gorge rise. She had seen plenty of evil and cruel things since learning about the vampire world, but this was beyond horrendous.

At last they came to a cliffside – a jagged rock from which a thousand-foot plummeted beneath them.

"We'll have to fly," Max said darkly. "Octavius, you take Stuart. Kal, can you…"

"Yes, moth…" Kalina stopped herself short. Calling Max *Mom* was still weird to her - "mother" was still the framed photograph of Mrs. Calloway that stood on her nightstand. "Max," she finished abruptly. "I can fly."

"Good," said Max. "We can't have you falling." She shuffled her feet to the edge of the cliff. Kalina looked down at the drop, her stomach plummeting. She had been able to fly before, in Mongolia. But would she be able to do it again now? After all, she'd been unable to fly after Molotov had weakened her…

She looked up at Max, but Max was looking straight ahead. "One…" Max began. "Two…"

It was now or never, Kalina decided. She

wasn't going to let anyone – especially Max – see her weak.

"Three!"

They all jumped in unison. Octavius was the first to break his fall, slowing his descent and gliding gracefully to the snowy bottom of the peak, Stuart in tow. Max, too, was able to control her fall. But Kalina felt the world grow blurry around her, the ground expanding beneath her as it grew ever-closer, gravity pulling and clutching at her...

She wasn't flying. Kalina's heart stopped. She was falling – falling a thousand feet, faster and faster...

Use the blood.

It was Max's voice – her mother's voice – echoing within her head. Kalina looked up, confused. Max had never used telepathy before.

Use the blood, daughter.

Kalina closed her eyes and concentrated.

Instantly she stopped falling, instead standing suspended in space. Her blood grew hot, warming her even in this chilling Alpine cold. And then she was slowly descending to earth, her body moving gracefully towards the others – floating down to join them as if she was being carried on wings.

"Well done," said Max, smiling. But when the others were out of earshot, Max's smile grew wry. "Don't be so afraid to ask for help when you need it. There's no shame in that. Next time, I'll carry you."

And with that, they continued through the snow banks, towards the ever-strengthening scent of the Carriers.

Chapter 15

From their new position at the bottom of the cliff, Kalina, Max, Octavius, and Stuart could better make out the terrain ahead of them. "Disgusting," Max was saying with a grimace. "I can sense it – we're getting closer. Wherever Mal left them, he left them so far down the mountain that they'd have to fly in order to get out. And I don't know a single Carrier under sixteen with those kinds of abilities. Unless..." She bit her lip.

"Unless what?" Kalina pressed further.

"Unless the kind of blood that we used on you and the other test babies – it's not like normal Life's Blood, we know that. But what if Mal thought that there was a chance that this special Life's Blood would manifest itself early. We know that adrenaline causes the Blood to reveal itself – maybe he thought that putting these girls in life-threatening situations would force their blood to respond." Max scanned the horizon. Before them was a vast expanse of pine trees lying across the valley, an enormous swarm of greenery. Kalina could smell the fragrance of pine fir in the end. It smelled like Christmas, Kalina thought grimly. She associated this smell with warmth, home, security. But for the girls out there, this was the smell of wilderness, or death. Her heart ached for these Carriers – taken away from their homes, from their lives. Most of them were missing parents, siblings (at the thought of *siblings*, Kalina felt tears stinging at the corners of her eyes), friends – fearing for their very lives. How could anyone, human or vampire, do something so unimaginably cruel?

She looked up at Octavius, who was staring out over the horizon. For so long she had thought of Octavius as nothing but her lover – a kind, strong man who happened to be a vampire. But now she regarded him with new fear. In the actions of this Malvolio – not to mention Molotov – Kalina saw a vampire capacity for cruelty she could never have imagined. Was Octavius, too, capable of such a deed? Was Jaegar? Stuart, she knew, had once been the Dark Knight, a killer of women and children as well as men. But she had never really understood the enormity of vampire potential for evil until now. Could her wonderful, kind Octavius, who always protected her through anything, be capable of such atrocities? The idea made Kalina shiver with horror. And if Kalina was beginning to take on vampire qualities, did that mean that one day she, too, would be capable of performing such acts as these?

"Fear not, my darling Kalina," Octavius said as they proceeded towards the forest, her thoughts evidently clear on her face. "Mal was not just a vampire. Even as a man, I have no doubt, Mal was cruel and immoral. Most vampires have terrible urges, but they know in their heart of hearts that such urges are wrong. Malvolio had no such compunctions. He never felt any guilt. And believe me when I tell you, Kalina, that vampires nearly *all* feel guilt, even the terrible ones. You needn't worry, my darling. This is not the natural outcome of vampire hunger. It is something far worse."

Blood Legacy: Pulse 6

They stopped short at the beginning of the forest as Max sniffed the air. "There," she said. "I can smell it. They're in there – not more than a ten-minute walk at most."

"You can sense their location so precisely?" Kalina looked at her mother in wonder. "From so far away, I mean? I can smell a generic Life's Blood in the air, but no more than that."

"When you've been working as long as I have," said Max, "you'll know that it's not a choice. Certain skills you'll need to learn – or die. Listen to me, Kalina – I sensed something at the hotel; I wasn't sure what. At first I thought it was just you I smelled – but now I'm sure it was something else."

"Another Carrier? An adult? Or one of the children..."

"I don't know," said Max. "The children wouldn't give off a scent this strong – but this new generation of Life's Blood isn't like the old one. The smell is stronger. It's hard to know what to expect."

"If they're out there," Octavius broke in, "we have to get to them quickly. They're likely as not to be held without food or water – we need to save them before they all starve or freeze to death. And let me tell you – I've seen men starve before. And I've seen men freeze, way back in Ancient Rome. It's not a pretty sight." He looked grimmer than Kalina had ever seen him.

Max led them into the forest, and at last they came to a concrete building, a windowless compound, the sight of which filled Kalina with trepidation. Now she too could sense the Life's Blood in the air. Even if the Carriers weren't there now, she knew they definitely had been here once; she could smell it. Max nodded – evidently she could smell it too.

The compound was dark – only a few electric lights swinging dimly from sockets gave any visibility at all to the damp, stifling corridors.

"This isn't right," Kalina whispered. The place seemed empty, even deserted. If the Carriers were there once, she knew, they had vanished long since. But something felt wrong about the place – very, very wrong. Kalina's spine was tingling with presages of danger. "We need to get out of here, Max," she whispered. "I have a bad feeling about this place..."

But Kalina was interrupted by a piercing scream that broke through their eerie silence like glass. It was the piercing scream of a young girl – a Carrier!

"Come on!" Kalina shouted as they ran towards the source of the voice, finding themselves in a small courtyard in the heart of the compound. "Let's go."

But they found no Carrier in the courtyard. Kalina felt a rough hand at the back of her neck – it was Octavius, holding her back. He grabbed Max and Stuart with the other hand. "Hold still," he growled. "It might be a trap. I smell vampires in the air."

No sooner had Octavius spoken than Kalina saw two vampires emerge into the courtyard, wearing Life's Blood rings on their fingers. They were newly-turned – Kalina could tell by the youthful, hungry look in their eyes. She wasn't too worried. The newer a vampire, the less powerful he was, and these vamps couldn't be more than a day or two old at the most. But Mal had been dead for some time. And if Mal hadn't turned them, who had?

Evidently, Octavius wasn't intimidated. He rushed forth into the courtyard, staking one vampire and picking up the other by the neck. Kalina winced as she heard the bones crack. He dragged the vampire into the shadows, wrenching the Life's Blood ring off his finger. "Better men than you have died for one of these," he hissed. "Now if you want your afterlife to continue more than twenty-four hours, tell me, fool – where are the Carriers?"

"The who?" The vampire spluttered. "The Carriers? Carrying what?"

"The ones with special blood," growled Octavius. "Tell me where they are, and I'll think about letting you live."

"I don't know anything!" The vampire yelped.

"The guy just told me to stay here, make sure nobody came by – I don't know anything."

Octavius squeezed him tighter by the neck. "Tell me what you know!" This time his voice was almost a roar. "Unless you want to die twice in two days. Don't think you can fight me, boy; I've lived for centuries."

"But I don't know anything!" The vampire's high-pitched voice reached the pitch of squeak. "Honest, I don't."

"I'll glamour you if I have to," Octavius spat. "Listen, those girls out there are cold, and alone, and hungry, and scared. And I'm not about to let anyone, especially an upstart pip squeak like you, stop me from saving their lives."

Kalina beamed with pride. How handsome Octavius was – even in anger, he exuded strength. He would fight for what he believed in, no matter what the cost.

"He knows nothing," said a familiar voice. "So

let him go. Kill him if you can, but it won't do you much good."

They whirled around to face Molotov, who stood before them with a sharp, wry grin on his face. "I suppose you're wondering why I bothered to use such a newly-turned vampire as a guard. Why, they're no better than cannon fodder, you doubtless thought – so weak you could kill them easily! But there's safety in numbers, friend Octavius." He stepped into the light, his red ring glimmering in the light of the sunset which now spread pink shadows over them all. "And you see, you can't fight off *everybody*."

Kalina and Stuart gasped. Behind Molotov, there appeared what looked like hundreds of vampires, stepping forth with grim expressions on their faces. Kalina's eyes opened wide with shock. "I recognize these people," she whispered. "That's the receptionist from the hotel, and that's the man I saw in the restaurant, and that's one of the children who was playing in the hotel lobby..."

Blood Legacy: Pulse 6

Stuart sighed. "I recognize more of them...when I went to the church, they were there...praying..."

At last realization dawned upon Kalina. "Why, he's transformed the whole village," she said in horror.

"That's right," Molotov shrugged. "You deprived me of my 'farm' in Mongolia, so I decided to take another route. I had my few remaining men turn the entire village in one night. Starting with your brother, and ending at the village school. Now the whole village of Aucaurgne-sous-Montaigne belongs to *me*." He grinned. "Let's see if you can take on all of them, shall we?"

Kalina looked wildly around. They were vastly outnumbered. And weak though they were, the newly-turned vampires all had a familiar look upon their faces.

They were hungry for blood.

Chapter 16

Kalina's heart began to pound. She quickly scanned the group of vampires that surrounded them, taking them all in. She was aghast at the horror of what she saw. She was used to seeing hardened, experienced vampires – vampires who had already killed many innocent men, women, and children, who had already lost their humanity. But these vampires *were* men, women, and children, and if they'd just been turned they might not even have fed themselves yet. These creatures, who stood before them, ready to sacrifice themselves in order to weaken them, were innocent – guilty only of being in the wrong place at the wrong time when Molotov decided to turn them all. Kalina felt sick. Would she have to stake women – would she have to stake *children?*

They're already dead, she told herself.

Blood Legacy: Pulse 6

Molotov's killed them. They're just shells. But were they? She looked over at Octavius. Whatever he was, he *wasn't* a shell. And these children – wasn't there hope that one day, a Carrier could turn them back to normal children, just as she had done with Stuart? How could she bring herself to kill any of them?

But from the grin on Molotov's face, she knew that this was part of his plan. She wouldn't hesitate to slay a trainer fighter, but killing any one of these newborn vampires before her would give her pause. Maybe enough time for them to kill her, instead.

"Why, you *monster*," Kalina breathed. "How could you?" She remembered the kindly smile of the hotel receptionist, the jovial grin of the old man whom she had spotted over drinks at the hotel dining room. Where were those smiles now? On these faces she could manage to see only cruelty and despair. "How could you do this – to all these people?"

Octavius stood silent and stony-faced before her. She knew what was going through his mind; she could feel it – their connection still strong enough for that. He was thinking of all the men *he* had turned over the years – Stuart and Jaegar and Aaron and so many hundreds more – and his eyes darkened with guilt and regret.

But one face among so many Kalina did not see, and this absence caused her to breathe a sigh of relief. Whoever else was out there, waiting to slaughter her, Justin was not among them. Had he been able to resist Molotov's call, after all? The thought gave her hope. If the Life's Blood in Justin was strong enough for him to break the hold Molotov had over him, then perhaps it would be able to counteract the effects of vampirism in him altogether!

But if Justin wasn't here, where was he? And where were the other Carriers? Kalina's heart began to beat faster. Night had only just fallen, and she couldn't tell if these new vampires had been out during the sunshine or not. They certainly weren't wearing rings. Did that mean that they had all drunk Carrier blood? Or were they only just waking now?

Blood Legacy: Pulse 6

Fear gripped her like a vice.

"Of all the despicable things I have known you capable of," growled Octavius in a low voice, "I never thought you would stoop so low as to do *this*."

"I will not let her live," Molotov glared at Kalina. "This *child*, this *girl*, has gotten the better of me once too often. She lives – she, who dared to cause the fall of my vampire stronghold, but not for long." He rushed forth, flying through the air, his hands outstretched as they clutched for Kalina's neck. But Octavius jumped in front of Kalina, pushing Molotov aside. His face was white with hot fury.

"How dare you!" Octavius cried, anger flooding through him. "I will never let you harm the woman I love ever again, mark my words. If I have to slaughter every last one of you to keep her safe, I will. But you will not hurt Kalina any more than you already have."

"What, you think you can order me around, you young upstart?" Molotov laughed, his eyes jeering with contempt. "You couldn't stop me if you tried. The girl's Life's Blood runs through my veins- a blood so strong that all other Life's Blood in the world is as nothing in comparison. And I nearly drained her dry. I doubt even your powerful rubies would stop me now – for those rubies were designed for vampires drinking far less blood than I have supped upon these past few days." He smiled, displaying bloody teeth. Kalina wanted to vomit at the sight – at the smell. SO much death... so much blood.

Molotov jumped to his feet, drawing himself up to his full, considerable height. "But I will not deign to fight you myself," said Molotov. "You must slaughter these *innocents* to get to me." He leaned back his head. "Vampires, *strike!*"

At his words, the whole horde of newly-turned vampires strode forth, their teeth bared. Kalina winced as she raised her stake. She could take on a few of them, but with only one full-fledged vampire in the pack, they were vastly outnumbered. Molotov had calculated all too well. He knew that neither she nor Max would be able to stake mere *children* – vampire or no. And that hesitation would cost them their lives.

Oh, Justin... Kalina thought desperately. *If you can hear me, wherever you are – please come to save us. Please break that hold that Molotov has over you. Don't let him win, Justin. You're stronger than that. I know you.* She prayed that their bond would let him hear her. If she could hear Octavius and Jaegar, after all, why shouldn't she be able to hear her brother, with whom she had a connection deeper than any romance? But there was no answer.

And now it was time to fight. Kalina tried to concentrate her attentions on staking only those who looked as if they had been turned as adults, but soon her efforts were proved fruitless. The only way to survive was to stake furiously – burying her ruby-wood into every approaching chest, regardless of sex or age. She felt ill – disgusted with herself, with Molotov – but she couldn't stop. It was her or them, and some adrenaline coursing through Kalina's veins convinced her that she had to stay alive.

There were too many of them. Their teeth flashed in the air; the smell of blood filled the courtyard. They kept coming; every time Kalina breathed a sigh of relief as one vampire staked into dust, ten more would come forth. Even Octavius was growing tired; Stuart, with nothing supernatural to give him strength, was all-but-collapsing. They were running out of energy, out of time. Sweat poured down their faces. It would all be over soon; they had only to wait...and to succumb.

And then they saw them. Kalina's heart began to race as she made out the figures at the corners of her eyes. Justin and Jaegar stood before her, their faces shining with bravery and courage, stakes in their hands. "Hello, sis," said Justin, with a smile. "I've come to rescue you."

Kalina's heart leaped within her chest. Had Justin really been able to fight off Molotov's influence? The smell of Life's Blood filled the air once again – Max, too, began sniffing. It was the same smell they'd experienced in the Inn – the mysterious Carrier who seemed to be following them wherever they were going.

And then it hit her. It was Justin. Kalina's
eyes opened wide with surprise. Justin – a Carrier?
Had Max's transfusion given him all the properties of
a real Carrier? Never before had a Carrier been
turned into a vampire – and it looked like Justin's
Life's Blood had served as an antidote against the
worst curses of vampire life. He was beautiful,
strong, and healthy-looking – he no longer had that
bloodthirsty look in his eye. The Life's Blood gave
him gravity, gave him strength. He had all the power
of a vampire, but none of the vampire's cruelty.
Kalina beamed with pride. How could she have
doubted that her big brother would have been strong
enough to fight off Molotov's influence? Justin had
always been strong enough to do the right thing –
she should have trusted that from the beginning.

And Jaegar, standing alongside him, was just
as beautiful. Kalina gasped with delight. She hadn't
seen Jaegar for so long – she had almost forgotten
just how handsome he was. As he stood before her
now, dressed in black silks, Kalina felt the familiar

weakening at her knees – she knew just how badly she wanted him. Even after everything. Even now. She had not realized until this moment just how much she missed him, missed his cocky smile, his easy arrogance. He grinned at her and suddenly Kalina's heart flooded with hope. Good old Jaegar. She could never bring herself to despair when he was around. In the glimmer in his eye she saw the possibility of escape.

"Come on, then!" Justin was shouting at Molotov. "You think you're so big and brave, turning defenseless humans? Well let me tell you something, *Master* – you don't control me any longer."

Jaegar materialized swiftly at Kalina's side, staking two newborn vampires as he did so. "I brought him home," he whispered, a smile spreading over his face. "Just as I promised I'd do for you, Kal. I'd do anything for you."

"Then he's okay?" Kalina's eyes filled with tears. She could hardly bear to let herself believe that Justin was safe, after all.

Blood Legacy: Pulse 6

"He's still a vampire," said Jaegar. "I couldn't do anything about that, of course. But I taught him how to fight Molotov's power over him. Usually only the most ancient vampires can fight vampire-glamour – but Justin's a natural. His Life's Blood – not to mention his love for you – made him able to resist Molotov's voice inside his head. He's free of Molotov's influence – at least for now."

Kalina watched in admiration as Justin effortlessly slew another three vampires, ash and dust crumbling all around him. "He's a strong man with an iron will," Jaegar said. "Almost as strong as his sister. When I found him, he was devastated, heartbroken. Just wanted me to stake him. But I talked to him. Tried to convince him that he could use his vampire powers for good, not evil. That he could use them to save you. And that made it easier for him to hold on to his humanity. To his good side. He loves you more than you know, Kalina. It's one thing for all of us to love you the way we do – we see you as a woman. But for Justin...you're *family*. It's a deeper bond than any of us will have." He sighed, and Kalina knew that he was thinking of the brother he had lost, of the bond that truly had been severed.

Jaegar caught Stuart's eye. "You're here too?" He gave Stuart a wry smile. "I didn't think it was safe to have humans in these parts."

"It's not," said Stuart grimly. "But it's worth the battle." He was bristling at Jaegar's presence. Evidently he, too, could see the attraction on Kalina's face. "I'll fight for Kalina whenever she needs help, vampire or not."

"Wow..." Jaegar's tone was sarcastic, but it betrayed genuine emotion. "I guess you are truly devoted, brother. You really do love her."

Kalina turned bright red and focused her attention on slaying the vampires – with Jaegar and Justin both fighting, they were falling swiftly and easily. She didn't want to hear this conversation.

"I do love her," said Stuart. "I thought that I never had a chance with her – but when I turned, it was all so clear to me. I did love her – I *do* love her now. I had so many dreams about what I'd do when I was human, what I'd do the second I turned...but when she left me, when we spent our first night together and she couldn't..." Stuart blushed and did not complete his sentence. "All those dreams became empty to me. I realized that even a human life is no true life without her."

"Spoken like a true romantic human," said Jaegar. To Kalina he spoke telepathically. *Is it true? That you and he never...*

None of your business. Kalina hoped that he would attribute the bright red spreading across her face to exhaustion, not embarrassment.

But you...didn't, did you? You can still turn back vampires? There is still hope?

Kalina said nothing. Memories were flooding back to her – memories of the agony she'd felt when Jaegar left, of how much she'd missed him, of how her whole body and soul had ached to run after him, to wrap her arms around him, to kiss him and promise him that *he* - he and nobody else – was the one she loved.

In the midst of her pain she had been sure he was the one. But did she feel that way now?

Jaegar, my love... She softened.

Kal, listen to me. His voice was so soft, so caressing, yet strangely insistent. *When we get through this, I'm going to show you just how much I miss you. I'm going to show you just how much I love you. I tried to forget you once you chose Stuart. I wanted to harden my heart against you, to control my emotions. I studied to be a stronger vampire – learning dreamwalking, how to counteract glamour, all these skills...and yet they amount to nothing when it comes to you. The second I see you, I melt – my hardened heart is as soft as a dove's wing. I could never turn my heart from you, Kalina. Not when I love you so. And even now, as we fight for our very lives, I can think only of kissing you...*

Molotov interrupted them as he stepped forth, evidently ready to fight now that his soldiers had largely been killed off. "So, we're all back together again," he sneered. "A nice little family reunion. And Kalina's *former* brother Justin. My protégée. He should have come straight to me when he turned. Don't dawdle, little boy, come to me now."

Justin stood motionless, glowering at Molotov.

"Never mind," Molotov spat. "If you're as weak a vampire as you seem, you're not worth having in my army anyway." He stepped back. "I have enough minions to do my bidding, besides."

Kalina and the others gasped in unison. Another group of vampire soldiers – these much stronger and older – stepped out of the shadow.

"The foot-soldiers have weakened you," sneered Molotov. "Now let's see if you have the strength to fight in the big leagues. These soldiers have not fed in weeks. They are hungry for human blood – and I spot *three* humans among you, two with delicious Life's Blood in their veins."

The vampires all licked their lips.

"Finally," said Molotov. "I will have my

revenge."

Chapter 17

The next group of vampires stumbled forward. Kalina looked up in confusion. These vampires seemed far more bloodthirsty and frightening than the last set – but yet their eyes were glazed-over, dull.

"What's going on?" Kalina whispered to Max. "Who are these vampires?"

Max pursed her lips. "I see what's happening," said Max. "Molotov's controlling them all with his mind. He's glamouring them – using their bodies to fight us instead of coming after us himself. He knows battle strategy – he's clever. But he doesn't want to risk his own cowardly skin. So he's glamoured these guys into doing his bidding."

Kalina's heart plummeted. Staking newly born vampires was one thing, but if Molotov was controlling them, she had no doubt that they would be far more dangerous. She saw that cruel glint in his eye – she knew he was all too brilliant when it came to battle-strategy. Willing to sacrifice these fifteen vampires to get to them.

Get the weak ones, Stuart and Jaegar traded glances. *The ones on whom the glamour is less strong. You can tell by the eyes.*

The two brothers immediately leaped into the fray, staking as many of the weaker-looking vampires as quickly as they could. "Oh, no you don't," Stuart was snarling at some of the vampires. "You're not going to get anywhere *near* Kalina, do you hear me." Max too jumped forward, fighting off two vampires at once, each of her muscular, lithe arms holding a glimmering red stake.

Kalina stepped forward, ready to fight, but she was stopped by a hand clapped hard over her mouth. She tried to scream, but the sound was muffled in her throat. "You've caused enough trouble for me, girl," Molotov had appeared behind her, another vampire standing at his shoulder. "Now at least I'll get some use out of you before I kill you." Kalina kicked and struggled, but Molotov and the other vampire held her down. Molotov pulled roughly on her wrist, revealing her bared arm. As Kalina screamed, her cries dying in her throat, Molotov sank a syringe-needle deep into her fore-arm, drawing copious amounts of blood into a plastic container. Kalina freed one arm and tried to push Molotov away, but it was no use. Pushing him away was like trying to push aside a boulder. He was massive, heavy, and immobile. Swiftly Molotov stuck another syringe into her arm, then another, and finally a third before at last Justin was able to wrench free from the vampire he was fighting.

"Get away from her!" A voice boomed out across the courtyard, as Justin's boots collided with Molotov's stomach, knocking him backwards. "You get away from my sister, you hear me?" Kalina looked up in surprise as Justin brandished a stake, sending his whole body spinning into Molotov's, knocking the older vampire into the snow. He raised his stake; Molotov, too, sprang to his feet, pulling a stake out of his cape. He threw it to the other vampire, an ancient-looking vampire with long blonde hair and a cruel expression.

"Drink!" Molotov shouted, and the vampire downed a gulp of Kalina's Life's Blood before rushing towards Justin, stake in hand.

"No!" Kalina cried, rushing to her feet. She was still reeling and dizzy from her second bout of blood loss in two days. "No, don't hurt him."

But it rapidly became clear to Kalina that she had no need to worry. Justin grabbed the vampire and began fending him off, his graceful body expertly challenging the vampire in hand-to-hand combat. Kalina had never seen anything this elegant, this acrobatic, since she had watched Molotov and Octavius fight in China. Her eyes opened wide. Justin was fighting like an ancient, seasoned vampire! He had only been turned less than twenty-four hours ago, but he fought with the confidence and power of a vampire who had been around for millennia. Was it the Life's Blood, Kalina wondered? Did a Life's Blood Carrier, turned into a vampire, have the ability to pick up vampire skills at a previously unknown pace? She beamed with admiration as she watched her brother fight. She should have known that Justin was special. As a human, he had always been braver and smarter than the other boys, stronger, more willing to stand up and fight for what was right. And now, as a vampire, Justin was one of the strongest fighters she'd ever seen. Kalina smiled. She was awfully glad to have someone like Justin as her brother, vampire or no.

The fighting continued – Justin and the ancient vampire relatively evenly matched. Kalina rushed forth, pulling the ruby-powder gun from the holster hidden in her jacket. "How about you leave my brother alone?" she cried, shooting the ruby powder straight into the vampire's heart. The vampire looked up at her with cold blue eyes, his expression turning to shock and awe as he exploded.

Justin looked up at her. "Nice work, Sis!"

Kalina rushed to Justin's side. She wanted nothing more than to hug him, to wrap him in her arms, but she held back. Molotov had vanished – and, knowing Molotov, who knew where he'd pop up next?

"Get back!" Octavius cried, and Kalina led Justin to behind where Octavius, Jaegar, Stuart and Max were fighting, leaning against one of the courtyard walls for safety.

"I'll rejoin the front lines," cried Justin, and he swapped places with Jaegar, who dropped back, rushing to Kalina and wrapping his arms around her

"Are you okay?" Jaegar held Kalina close. "How are you doing, Kal? That bastard took so much of your blood – I was so worried..." He scowled. "I could feel it as if it were I who were being drained. I felt your pain, your loss. That was when I knew no matter how much I tried to close my heart against you, I would never be able to truly turn my back on you. My pain is your pain. Your pain is mine. We are connected – a connection that not even my foolish

- 191 -

jealousy could break. I would rather let my heart shatter a hundred times, staying at your side and watching you love another, than let you get hurt again. I cannot bear being apart from you, Kal. I cannot bear it!" His eyes were so full of love, so full of adoration. Kalina too felt her own heart begin to melt. She wanted nothing more than to give him what he wanted, to succumb to him, to kiss him. But she couldn't let Stuart or Octavius see – she knew how it would hurt them. She took his hand and pulled him around a corner, away from the vampires' gaze.

"What are you doing, Kal?" Jaegar looked confused. "Where are we going?"

"Right here," Kalina whispered. She pushed him up against the walls of the corridor, pressing her lips against his. There was so much she wanted to say with that kiss – so much she wanted to explain. How much she loved him, how much she missed him, how much she had longed for him in his absence. *It hurt so much, Jaegar – when our connection broke down. When I couldn't reach you. I thought you were dead – or that you never wanted to see me again. I dreamed of you every night, Jaegar. You've always meant so much to me. You've changed my life in ways you'll never know. You've brought me passion, excitement, thrill. I was so afraid – out of all of you – I was so afraid I'd lose you after what happened with Stuart...*

Then it's true? You do care for me most, after all of them?

He searched her face, anger and passion both hot in his gaze. *I love you, Kal, and I always will. I know your choice is a difficult one, but deep down I know that you won't let yourself settle for anyone else until you've given it a shot with me – until then, you'll never be sure. You'll always be wondering, waiting...I'm telling you, Kal. You don't love Octavius and Stuart the way you love me. I care for them, too, but they're not right for you. You and me, we're like two sides of a coin – we belong together. Evenly matched. Equals.* He leaned in and kissed her. *When we get through this, when we go get the Carriers, I want you to tell me those three little words. I want you to tell me that I'm the man for you, and nobody else.*

Kalina felt herself swoon. How did Jaegar always have this effect on her? Once again, she thought, he was looking more human – just as he had done last time they kissed – his milky-white skin growing rosy and dark, even as she grew paler. Then, before she could refuse, Jaegar bit his wrist and pressed the wound to her lips. Greedily, instinctively, she began to drink.

"You've lost so much blood," said Jaegar. "You're starting to look weak. We need our strength if we're going to fight the rest of these vampires off. Drinking a human like Stuart won't quench your thirst. You'll need to drink from me, to have the blood of a vampire in you."

She was sucking harder, now, her mouth stained with blood, overwhelmed by her hunger and her desire. And then she was kissing him – they were bruising each other with each passionate, rough kiss, their desire stronger than ever.

"Justin," she whispered, pulling away. "You

saved him." She gave him a dazzling smile that left him floored. "You protected him – freed him from Molotov's curse."

Jaegar shrugged. "I didn't do much," he said. "He had that strength in him already. It was the power of Life's Blood, which can counteract even the effects of a maker's will. He's a strong person... Justin. He always was. And while he was your brother in life, and always will be, now he is my brother in blood, and I will protect him with my life."

"Thank you," Kalina whispered, kissing him once again. "Thank you for taking care of Justin for me. I'll never be able to thank you enough..."

"I know how you can thank me."

"We have to save the Carriers first." Kalina stopped short as the idea hit her. "You said *when we get the Carriers*. Do you know where they are?"

Jaegar nodded. "Yes," he said.

"Where are they?" Kalina asked.

Blood Legacy: Pulse 6

"Not here, that's for sure," said Jaegar. "We were here earlier – didn't find them. But we figured out where they were. I'll lead you there."

"That's wonderful, Jaegar!" Kalina's eyes shone brightly.

"Yes," said Jaegar. "But first we have to get out of here alive. I'll help Justin against Molotov directly – you deal with the minions. Use your ruby gun – it has a good range." He kissed her one last time, and Kalina almost passed out with desire. "Now let's go back to the battle."

Chapter 18

They ran back into the fray, Jaegar rushing over to help Justin fend off Molotov. With Jaegar's blood pumping through her, Kalina felt stronger – more powerful. Adrenaline was coursing through her veins. She had reloaded the gun with more rubies; another, larger, machine gun, outfitted with wooden stakes, was slung over her shoulder. She threw the second gun to Stuart. "Over here!"

Stuart caught it deftly, looking up at her in surprise. She could see the exhaustion on his face; he was the only one of the group without supernatural powers, and it was starting to take his toll. His skin was covered in scratches and bruises – lacerations that Kalina was ashamed to admit made her hungry when the smell reached her nostrils – and dark circles hung under his eyes. "When there's an opening, take it. Get out of here. Jaegar thinks he knows where the Carriers are – they're not here. Just get out safely."

Stuart nodded, his expression grave. His lips were pale and bloodless; his skin was yellowing. They'd been fighting for hours, Kalina knew, with no food or water – Stuart wasn't going to be able to keep it up much longer. Max and Octavius had taken over the front lines for the time being; Max was swinging her sword, slashing vampires in two – Octavius, rather, stuck to using his bare hands, ripping vampires' heads from their bodies. Kalina looked at them both in wonder. Yet this time it was Max who caught her eye. Max was so strong, Kalina thought wistfully, so brave. Would she ever be as strong, as heroic, as Max? Max was never overwhelmed by her emotions; Max was never stunned by desire. Max was in control. Why couldn't she, too, gain control? Kalina sighed. And yet how could she keep control at all when Octavius was in the room? He was like a king among vampires, Kalina thought – even in the heat of battle, he maintained his noble countenance; his body was always lithe and graceful, always beautiful. Even now, some of the newborn vampires were breaking Molotov's hold over them – too afraid to fight a battle they would surely lose.

"Max! Octavius!" Kalina called out. She shifted to telepathy, anxious not to be overheard by the vampires. *Listen up,* she said. *The Carriers aren't here. We need an exit strategy – now. On the count of three, run over to me and Stuart; Stuart's going to blast us out of here.*

Octavius gave Kalina a tiny, almost imperceptible, nod.

One – Kalina tightened her grip on her gun – *Two* – Max picked up her gun – *Three.*

Immediately Octavius and Max sprang to Kalina's side, shooting the stakes from their guns in unison. Fifteen vampires crumbled into dust in unison.

Kalina looked up. The fight had moved from the courtyard to the corridors; Molotov had sent the newborn vampires to trap them indoors. But why? And then it hit her. The Life's Blood in the new vampires would be wearing off by now – especially if he'd only been able to use a small amount for each vampire. Exposure to sunlight would kill them.

They can't go back into the sunlight. Kalina looked at Max. *We need to bring the sunlight to them – the blood's wearing off.*

Octavius added in. *There's a rear courtyard – I saw it when I was reloading my weapon. It's covered by a dark glass dome. If we can get them in there and bring the roof down...*

Then it'll go down on all of us, too! Max's voice vied with Octavius' in her head. *And if we can't shatter the dome, we'll lose our strategic advantage. We can't take them all at once; we have to use skill, not strength.*

It's worth the risk, Octavius decided. *Get to the rear courtyard...bring the ammo. Kalina, you get Justin and Jaegar...let them know the plan. We'll lure the vampires into the courtyard and then hit.*

Kalina nodded. As Stuart and Max began

carrying bags of ammunition and rubies into the rear courtyard, Octavius sauntered up to her. He wrapped her in his arms, his eyes shining with love. "I love you, Kalina," he whispered. "This whole battle – watching you fight...I've been waiting to say it to your face this whole time. I'm so proud of you, of your bravery. I need you to be strong now, Kalina. To be brave. What I'm about to ask of you is dangerous. But it's the only way."

"Anything, Octavius!" She felt her heart beat faster.

"We need to cut you – just enough to fill the dome with your scent. If you bleed onto the ground, the vampires will rush into the dome in search of you; we can get them all in there before anybody notices you've already gone. But you'll need to bandage yourself up immediately afterwards. If it doesn't drive me wild, the smell might be too much for Jaegar or Justin." He pulled her close. "If any of us lose control, Kalina – you know what you need to do..."

Blood Legacy: Pulse 6

"I'd never stake you, Octavius."

"I do not know the limits of my strength," Octavius murmured, "but, my girl, you're certainly testing them." His eyes penetrated deep into her; she could feel his hunger as if it were her own. He pulled her in for a kiss – a kiss of such savage tenderness that Kalina knew that Octavius, too, feared it would be the last time.

Kalina signaled to Justin and Jaegar, who appeared immediately. *Go through the courtyard – meet me at the back.*

One by one, they all rushed to the room on the other side of the domed courtyard. *Here goes nothing,* Kalina thought, biting into her own wrist. The smell of her blood filled the air. Even from a distance, she could see Octavius' face change; the second he inhaled her smell, his customary serenity was displaced by a look of voracious desire. Would he be able to keep control?

She pressed her wrist to the ground, letting the free-flowing blood soak the earth.

"I smell it!" she heard one of the vampires cry. "The girl's down – she's bleeding. Let's get her!"

"Looking for blood?" Octavius crowed. "Go find it, then!"

Kalina rushed to the other side of the dome, tearing her shirt and fashioning a bandage from the rags. She watched as all of Molotov's vampires ran into the courtyard, sniffing and shouting wildly. "Where is she?" "I can smell her blood!" "She's hiding!" "Where?"

Kalina looked at Max. "Now?"

"Now," Max nodded, aiming her gun square at the roof. Stuart and Octavius picked up their weapons. "Fire!"

Ten stakes went flying through the air; they pierced the glass of the ceiling, which fell apart like struck crystal. A wild wail went up from the vampires as sunlight flooded the dome; Kalina felt nauseous as the smell of burning flesh reached her nostrils. One by one, the vampires burned into nothingness.

Blood Legacy: Pulse 6

Kalina was bleeding harder than she thought; the blood was soaking through the bandage. "Come on," she said, "Let's run." But a pair of hands was already upon her, grabbing her savagely, pulling her out into the snow.

"What the...Octavius?" His fangs were exposed; he was breathing heavily. She had never seen him look so bestial before – so in thrall to his own desires. The past few days had only tantalized him; he craved her more than ever. She could see it in his eyes – see for the first time a danger she was only just beginning to understand...

"Kalina," Octavius gasped, fighting his instincts. "I don't know if I can control it..." He was shaking. "I can't – your scent, the adrenaline, this feeling..."

Yes, Kalina thought joyously! This was the moment. At last he would take her, drink her blood – at last she would turn him. "Then don't fight it," she whispered. "Take me, Octavius. I want you to want me – I've waited so long."

His fangs extended further; he pushed her down into the snow. Kalina pushed back her hair, baring her neck for him, waiting for him to bite, and craving his kiss.

Octavius groaned softly. But he did not bite her, giving his lips over instead to fervent, fevered kissing of her neck, her lips. She opened her mouth to him, her heart throbbing faster still. "Go on," she whispered.

"Oh, Kalina," he moaned. "You tempt me too much." He sprang to his feet, turning his back to her. "I can't do this..."

In a moment she too was on her feet, running to Octavius, wrapping her arms about his neck, kissing him. "Please, Octavius," she cried. "I'm yours."

"Don't make me do this," his voice shook. "There are Carriers to be found, Carriers who need us – to bring them back to their families. There's Molotov."

Blood Legacy: Pulse 6

"We have Max...Justin..."

"Jaegar?" Octavius looked back at Kalina, jealousy in his eyes. "Or will you turn him?"

"If I can turn more than one vampire," Kalina began, "then I can turn you both. Give you both what you want. But I know what I want, Octavius and I want to be with you..."

Octavius scoffed. "If your feelings for Jaegar and Stuart are that strong," he said, "you shouldn't risk trying it on me. I don't want one-third of your heart, my darling. I want it all." He strode back towards the others, leaving Kalina shaking and hurt. The compound was all but empty now; the vampires were turned to char and cinders.

Kalina fought back the tears. Octavius would give in someday, she told herself. She just had to give him time...

Justin was fighting off the last of the minions with two stakes; Jaegar was brandishing his gun to pick out any survivor. In the distance, Molotov appeared, carrying something in front of him. Kalina looked closer.

"He's using another vampire as a shield," she said. "We can't get to him without staking the other vamp."

Justin fired a shot, but it was no use. The stake went straight into the heart of the other vampire, sending him crumbling into dust.

"We've got you now!" Justin called.

Molotov smirked. "You think I lived this long by being a fool? You'll never get me, boy. I'm your Maker!" And with that, he vanished – leaving nothing but empty space where he had been.

"What the..." Kalina blinked. "How did he do that?"

Octavius did not look at her. "He's getting stronger – turning must have done that to him. Only the strongest vampires can simply disappear like that. They straddle the line between dead and undead – they can harness the powers of Death at will."

Kalina frowned. "We should have finished him off..."

"He'll only get stronger," Stuart sighed.

"He'll rebuild his army. First he turns a whole village – what's next, a city? He's willing to turn thousands if it means holding us off."

"Kalina!" Justin turned to his sister. It was the first time she'd been able to touch him since he'd turned. She rushed into his arms, letting the tears flow freely.

"Don't worry, Kal. I've accepted it. What I am. Who I am. I'm living on vampire wine – Jaegar showed me how. They're going to look after me. Take me back to the Vineyard. Use my medical knowledge to try to improve vampire wine, make it stronger...and if I'm a vampire, it means I might be able to heal my patients. Use my blood for good. And hey, if I don't need to eat, I can use that money to pay off my student loans, right?" He smiled weakly.

'I'll work on looking through the Doctor's paper's, figuring out the formula for Life's Blood. I've got more than a lifetime to find the formula now. You haven't lost me, Kal. I've just got more useful, that's all!" He hugged her tighter. "It wasn't your fault, Kal. It wasn't anybody's fault. I knew the risks when I signed up for this gig..."

"When I thought I'd lost you..." Kalina sobbed. "It hurt so much. I was so worried."

"Listen, Kal," Justin grinned. "You don't have to worry about me anymore. For the first time, I can take care of myself. And that means you can live the life you've always wanted without worrying about keeping me out of danger."

"I love you, Justin," Kalina whispered. "I thought I'd lose you if you turned – but now I have you back, and I feel like the luckiest girl in the world. You'll always be my big brother."

"Just what you need, huh, Kal?" Justin joked. "Another vampire man in your life."

Blood Legacy: Pulse 6

Octavius broke in. "We've spent enough time here," he said. "Jaegar, Kalina told me that you possibly have information about the Carriers?"

Jaegar nodded. "I heard through the grapevine. Molotov wanted to stall us – he sent us out here on a wild goose chase to get his revenge. But Mal...he always knew there was one place we wouldn't look – a place so simple it escaped us..."

"I don't understand," Kalina began.

Justin's eyes widened. "I think I do. Where do you normally keep something you don't want found..."

And then it hit her. "In the most obvious place possible. In your own backyard."

"Right," said Jaegar. "Because that's where they've been all along. Rutherford, California."

Chapter 19

After Kalina, Max, and the vampires returned to the hotel and packed their things, it was time to head off again. Stuart commissioned his private jet once more, and the group prepared to return to Rutherford. Kalina's excitement was tinged with frustration. While she was relieved to know at last the location of the Carriers, she was furious with herself for not having recognized Mal's gambit earlier. She should have guessed that Mal had been playing tricks on them all along – planting false information and perhaps even false Carrier blood to lure them to Switzerland.

And all along, the Carriers had been in Rutherford! Kalina couldn't believe it. But deep down, Kalina was relieved. She was willing to travel to wherever it took to get the Carriers, but she was exhausted; to return to Rutherford meant, at least, returning home. The others were tired, too, and Kalina knew that the thirteen-hour flight would provide some much-needed rest for all of them. Stuart was up front, directing the pilot. Octavius, Jaegar, and Justin were all asleep on leather sofas, at last resting from the wounds and scars of battle.

"I brought you some tea," Stuart returned to the cabin. He sat down next to Kalina, his hand touching hers. "I've gotten used to human food now." He laughed sadly. "But all the caffeine in the world won't take this exhaustion away. I'm not designed to fight like a vampire anymore, Kalina; my body can't handle it." He turned to her, gazing into her eyes, his own expression filled with sadness. "You don't have to say anything, Kalina," he whispered softly. "I've always felt it. And now I feel it – stronger than ever. I know I can't keep holding you back, keep standing between what you are and what you feel. You're becoming vampire – a transformation I don't even understand – but a transformation that's keeping you away from me. I'll always love you, Kalina, but I'm a human now. All these experiences have made it clear to me that I'm not cut out for this life anymore. I'll always be there for you – but I know you're not ready for a life with me. And to be honest, Kalina, I'm not sure you'll ever be. You're not built for the kind of life I thought I wanted. And I'm no longer capable of the kind of life..." He kissed her fingers. "My human body won't be able to take much more of this – fighting vampires, hunting down Molotov. And if I last another few weeks at this – I'll give up all the good I hope to do. Settling down. Working for peace. Atoning for what I've done." He held her close.

"I wanted to marry you, Kalina. To be *with* you. To have a family with you. But if I can't do that, I need to go back to my original calling. Not to be a Protestant pastor – married, with a family. But to give my life to God more fully than that. To become a priest as priests were when I was a child, when we were Catholics. I will swear off that kind of love with any woman – better nobody than anyone who isn't you. You'll always be the only girl for me, Kalina. And I'll always be there for you. Whatever you need."

"I know," Kalina said softly. "I can feel it. We're

connected now – by Life's Blood. You'll always be a part of me." She stroked his face. His skin was rough. "Is this really what you want?"

Stuart grimaced, trying to hide the pain. "You know what I want," he whispered hoarsely. "But Fate has chosen to deny me..." He took a deep breath. "And so I'll have to accept it. I'll find another path. Not everyone needs to be married, right?"

"Oh, Stuart!" Kalina squeezed his hand; he squeezed hers right back. But she couldn't say anything to change his mind – in her heart of hearts, she knew what he said was true. She could never truly love him – not while she was so deeply, so madly and passionately in love with another. But, she knew, no matter what happened, she would always be Stuart's friend.

She fell asleep halfway over the Atlantic, allowing herself to doze off at last. When she woke, she felt a familiar warmth pressing alongside her.

"Morning, Kal!" Jaegar was stroking her hair softly. He had been watching her sleep. He pulled her into him, his blue eyes full of love. "Did I ever tell you, Kal, you look so peaceful when you sleep. Vampires – we rarely see such a peaceful look. Seeing the way your eyelashes curl so delicately against your face. The way your chest goes up and down – just like that! - when you breathe." He smiled, almost embarrassed at this display of emotion. "I love...oh, heck, Kal," he pulled her closer. "I'm not good at this. I don't know what to say. All I know is that I love everything about you." He leaned in, kissing her.

Kalina looked around, embarrassed. But Stuart was gone – evidently up front with the pilot again – and Octavius too was absent. Max and Justin were having a conversation, their backs turned to Jaegar and Kalina. There was nobody to stop her.

Kalina kissed Jaegar back, feeling their chemistry ignite, while moving to the back of the plane. "Let's be alone together," Jaegar whispered with urgency. She wanted him now more than ever; ever since his blood had begun to flow in her veins, she wanted to kiss him, to devour him, to consume him; her body was addicted to his. Jaegar didn't even have to speak. It was clear from his expression just what he wanted. Her. She could feel his muscles ache with restraint; all he wanted, she knew, was just what she wanted – for him to throw her down onto the floor and take her, at last.

"Jaegar," Kalina sighed. "I missed you so much when you were gone. I..." But Jaegar silenced her with a kiss, lightly biting her upper lip.

"I swear, Kal," he breathed, unbuttoning his shirt. "I want you so badly – if I can't...I'll stake myself, Kal..."

"Don't worry..." Kalina whispered, running her fingers through his hair. "I want you too."

"No!" Jaegar pulled away suddenly. "No, stop!"

"What is it?" Kalina looked up in confusion. Jaegar had never reacted like this before.

"I can't – I can't get so close – and then stop....I won't be able to stop myself this time. I can feel it. If we get close, we'll go all the way. I can't keep waiting, torturing myself, getting so close to the object of all my desires only to lose it. I want you so badly, Kalina, that it's killing me. And that scares me." His eyes darkened; they were smooth and black like slate. "And thinking of you with Stuart – or with Octavius – it kills me. It makes me want to kill *them*."

"Don't talk like that," Kalina stroked his arm.

"I can't take it anymore, Kal!" Jaegar's face was filled with a mixture of love and rage as he stormed off.

Kalina remained in the back of the plane, shocked. What had happened? Her vampire lovers were always willing to take it slow before, to respect her space, to respect the time it was taking for her to make her decision. But now she saw a different side of Jaegar. A hungry, impatient side – a side that frightened her.

About ten minutes later, when Kalina had returned to the cabin, Jaegar again sat down alongside her. He took her hands in his and kissed her. "I'm sorry, Kal," he said. "I don't know what's gotten into me. Something about your blood – about our connection – it's making me crazier than usual. My blood's acting up again."

"Don't worry about it," Kalina blushed. How could she blame Jaegar for being jealous, when after all she couldn't bear to make the decision that would end all rivalry forever? "Hey, I don't mind when you lose control around me." She tried to make a joke, but as she spoke, she felt the full heat of her desire coursing through her. She could see that Jaegar felt the same way.

Out of the corner of her eye, Kalina spotted Octavius emerging from the back of the way. He looked smug, sated. A drop of blood lingered on his lips as he leaned back comfortably on the level chair. One of the flight attendants, a slim blonde girl in her early twenties whom Kalina had not seen before, emerged just after him, conspicuously covering up her neck with her scarf. She was beautiful; Kalina couldn't help noticing, with snowflake-white skin and blonde hair, and a complexion so perfect as to be almost doll-like. She was smiling at Octavius, and Octavius was smiling back.

Kalina couldn't restrain her jealousy. Octavius never smiled at just a meal like that. There had to be something more between them.

"Relax," Jaegar patted Kalina's leg. "Don't worry about it. Believe me, the last thing I want to do is reassure you about Octavius – I'm jealous that you're jealous – but I'll be honest: that girl means nothing to him. She meant nothing to me. She's just...a good source of blood, that's all."

"Then you two...?"

"We ran low on vampire wine," Jaegar explained quickly. "I don't even remember her name. Alice or something? Maybe it was Suzanne."

Kalina had to stifle a laugh. "Alice or Suzanne?" she said. "How do you even *get* from one to the other?"

"I told you, I couldn't remember. I was hungry."

Blood Legacy: Pulse 6

"Listen, Jaegar." Kalina rubbed her hand up and down his thigh. "Soon, my love, you won't have to dine on waitresses and flight attendants any longer. You'll be able to get your meals from me."

Jaegar's eyes widened with surprise. "You mean..."

She nodded.

"I meant what I said," Jaegar said. "When I said I wanted to show you how much I loved you. I only wanted the chance. To woo you the right way. To be the romantic one for change, instead of the unreliable bad boy. To deserve you. I want to give you everything you wanted. Fly you to Paris, take you on a gondola ride in Venice – everything your heart desires, Kal. Won't you give me that chance?"

Jaegar leaned in to kiss Kalina, but he was interrupted by a loud *ahem*. Kalina and Jaegar looked up to see Octavius, who was glaring at both of them through dark eyes. Kalina knew that look – it was the raw, furious force of true passion. He was jealous – more jealous than he would ever admit;

only his honor and his oath prevented him from staking Jaegar there and then.

"I need to speak with you, Kalina," Octavius said stiffly.

Kalina sprang to her feet, embarrassed. "Look, Jaegar," she said. "I need to talk to Octavius for a second," she said. "I'll be back."

Chapter 20

Octavius led Kalina to the back of the plane. Before they could even sit down, Kalina felt Octavius' lips hungry upon hers, kissing her with abandon, his hands deftly caressing her body, her curves – all of her...

Kalina pulled back in surprise. Only hours before, Octavius had angrily rejected her advances. But now he was all over her, kissing her with a sheer passionate abandon she thought was lost forever. His touch was electric; she struggled to shut down her telepathic connection with Jaegar. She couldn't let him know that she still felt this way about Octavius, that she still wanted him so much. But something was strange. Octavius' kisses were not just rough, but brutal – demanding. Overwhelming. Kalina tried to force herself to respond, but instinct pulled her back. Something felt wrong.

"What's going on, Octavius?" she asked.

"I've been thinking," Octavius said. "I've decided that it's not worth the heartbreak any longer. I want you. I want you now. Totally, completely. To spend the rest of eternity with you on your terms."

They were the words Kalina had been longing to hear. But something felt wrong – she couldn't bring herself to believe them. His eyes were not loving, but cruel; and they were vaguely red and bloodshot. Kalina thought back to Jaegar in the back of the plane – were his eyes not a little red, too? Kalina sniffed the air – it smelled of nothing but vampires and Carriers, the same familiar smell.

What could have happened to Jaegar and Octavius to make them both so passionate – so frightening – in such a short space of time? And then, from the curtain dividing the back of the plane from the main cabin, Kalina caught a glimpse of the flight attendant. She was lovely, to be sure – but there was something else about her, too. Something special.

Blood Legacy: Pulse 6

Kalina pulled away from Octavius, striding towards the girl. The smell was faint but as she grew closer to the flight attendant the feeling in her blood was unmistakable. Did this woman have Carrier blood in her? The smell was almost impossible to make out – so subtle that Octavius and Jaegar would both fail to realize it, to realize they had been drinking the blood of a Carrier.

Kalina strode over to the woman. "Excuse me," she said quietly, "I'm sorry, but I'll need you to come with me. We have an emergency that needs dealing with out back."

"Of course," the woman nodded. She followed Kalina to a secluded part of the plane. "What's going on?"

"What's your name?" Kalina looked the woman up and down. Yes, Kalina thought bitterly – she *was* beautiful. Certainly beautiful enough to have attracted both Octavius and Jaegar. But she couldn't let herself be jealous now.

"Suzanne-Alice," the woman said. "Is there a

problem with the plane, ma'am?"

Kalina shook her head. "It's not about the plane," she said. "It's about what happened...you know..."

"With *them*?" Suzanne-Alice raised an eyebrow as she looked over to Octavius and Jaegar.

"Have you had a blood test done before, Suzanne-Alice?" Kalina's heart was beginning to pound.

"Ages ago – when I was a kid. I think I was a type O or something – I don't know. It's probably in some medical file somewhere..."

Kalina frowned. It looked like this girl definitely didn't know about her own Carrier blood – she clearly wasn't lying.

"And your mother?" Kalina pressed further. "What type was she?"

Suzanne shrugged. "As if I knew!" she scoffed. "My mother was a drug addict who left me with a foster family in Basel – I never knew her..."

"And you've been...with vampires before?"

Suzanne smiled and colored slightly. *"Non,"* she said, her Swiss accent becoming more evident as she spoke. "Just these two handsome fellows – they explained everything to me. It is safe, I know."

Kalina felt her skin prickle with envy. She'd never felt such jealousy before. She'd tried so hard to give Octavius her Life's Blood – but this girl, who didn't even *know* them – who didn't even know her own strength, had let them feed from her. No wonder they had both been acting strangely. She knew the effect that Life's Blood had upon a vampire who did not drink from his true love. It caused raging madness – a loss of control. Kalina shuddered as she remembered how both Stuart and Jaegar had behaved when under the influenced. She couldn't bear going through that again.

Max, who had been listening silently to the conversation, took Suzanne by the hand. "Listen to me," she said. "I'm going to have to explain everything to you..." She led Suzanne away to sit her down leaving Kalina alone with Justin. "Kalina, I'll run some tests. I brought a kit with me...Suzanne, come with me."

"I don't understand," Justin said. "You think we've got another Carrier on board?"

Kalina began to feel nervous. Justin would be able to control himself around Kalina's blood – but would his desire for another Carrier outweigh his good intentions? He wasn't as strong as Jaegar or Octavius at controlling his emotions yet. "We'll have to do some tests," she said, watching as Justin's eyes followed the girl's beautiful frame down the aisle of the plane, darkening with desire.

"I'm going to go sit down," said Justin.

Octavius came over to Kalina. His eyes had grown redder; his expression was even more passionate than it had been. He pulled her aside once again, pressing his lips against her fingers, sending thrill after thrill through her as his tongue darted over her knuckles, over the tips of her fingers.

Blood Legacy: Pulse 6

He leaned in, murmuring throatily: "Remember when we were at the castle, my love? Remember how we shared that tub? So warm, the water. So caressing. I want to do that again, Kalina – but this time I'd like to do far more than hold you..." He kissed her ear, beginning to nibble greedily on the lobe. Kalina closed her eyes and sighed. Perhaps the Life's Blood wasn't turning Octavius evil, she thought hopefully – perhaps it was only taking away his inhibitions...

"You drank from Suzanne..." Kalina began.

Octavius smiled at her. "Why? Jealous?"

"Yes," Kalina flushed.

"Silly Kalina – you don't need to be jealous. You know what I want. You and only you."

Max returned without Suzanne. She took Kalina aside, whispering into her ear. "I've done the tests, Kalina," she said steadily. "She's not a full Carrier. But she has some Carrier blood in her – perhaps a relative, perhaps a distant cousin. Blood not as strong as yours or mine – but just a drop of

Life's Blood..." she sighed. "Don't let any of the vampires drink from her until this is sorted out."

"Too late," said Kalina.

"I see," Max looked worried. "Then keep an eye on them. Won't you? You know them better than I – you'll know if they start acting...strange."

"Do you think she's one of the Carrier children?" Kalina asked. "Are they all half-Carriers, like her? That could be why we've had trouble smelling them out."

Max sighed. "I don't know," she said. "You were all experimental. None of us knew what to expect. Your blood was a combination of mine and the Calloways' serum – others injected with the serum had little to no Carrier blood at all...the serum that finished the Doctor's work."

At the mention of the Doctor, Kalina remembered the metal box she had found at the Doctor's residence in China. She reached into her bag and showed it to her mother. "I found this a few weeks ago," said Kalina. "At the Doctor's residence, after we fought Molotov. Do you know what it is?"

Max shook her head. "Open it."

But before Kalina could do so, Jaegar walked over, interrupting them. "I've been going through some of the papers we recovered from the compound," he said. "A map of Rutherford – marked with an X. It looks like Mal was planning to bring the girls to Switzerland after all – once he'd narrowed down the most likely Carriers. He was going to drink the rest..."

Kalina felt sick again. Yet as she looked into Jaegar's eyes, she felt sicker still. His irises had turned bright red. His desire was palpable – mingled with danger. He wanted her, she knew – and he was going to take her. Right here, right now. It was no longer a look of love. It was simply savage obsession.

"Kalina!"

At the sound of her name, Kalina whirled around. Octavius stood before her, his eyes also bright red – his face also bestial in its hunger.

She gulped. These weren't the men she knew – kind, gentle, loving vampires. The Life's Blood had done its work.

Their humanity was hanging by a thin thread. She was standing between two Life's Blood monsters.

And they both wanted her.

Epilogue

Kalina's heart was pounding. If both Octavius and Jaegar were under the influence of Life's Blood, then they were both dangerous. Forget about saving the other Carriers, Kalina thought as she blanched in terror – right now, she'd have to focus on saving herself. She was trapped 38,000 feet in the air with two vampires hopped up on Life's Blood. There was no way out. She remembered what had happened last time – how Jaegar had turned so cruel, so evil. Would he turn that way again? And Octavius? She looked back and forth from one to the other, horrified. How could she bear to lose either one of them?

"Get Suzanne-Alice out of here," Kalina said, looking over at Max.

Max nodded. "Go sit with Stuart, Suzanne.

Wait at the front of the plane – in the cockpit. Lock the doors and don't open them to anybody but us."

Suzanne-Alice looked confused but she complied silently. Before Kalina could say anything, however, Jaegar was at her side. His eyes were filled with lust and longing. He turned his penetrating gaze onto her, and Kalina felt chills running up her spine. "Kal..." he whispered. "Something's going on – something's wrong. I'm losing control."

Kalina knew the first thing to do was to get him out of view of Octavius. They were dangerous enough to her right now, but she imagined – if they were as prone to jealousy in this condition as she suspected – that they would be more dangerous still to each other. "Just go sit down," she said to Jaegar, trying to pat his arm reassuringly. "I'll come over in a second."

Max was examining the box Kalina had given her. "I've tried the box," she said shortly. "It won't open – it's stuck."

"You think it needs a key?"

Blood Legacy: Pulse 6

Max shook her head. "Doubt it," she said. "The problem isn't a key – it's...something else. Something deeper. Magic, I should say."

"Magic?" Kalina whirled around to face her mother, surprised.

"The inscription on the box – it's classical Chinese; I can read it. It says it right here – *The rights of Life's Blood are strong. Strength is sealed by age.* Presumably it means that only an ancient vampire can open the box."

Kalina – Kalina was interrupted by the voice of telepathy in her head. Jaegar was sitting as she had asked him to – but his thoughts were less compliant than his body. *You look quite delectable, my darling.* His voice was cruel. *I want you right now – right here. I'm this close to simply taking you – even here. In front of everybody. I've waited and waited for you, and you've denied me too long..."*

Kalina colored but said nothing. She didn't want to panic Max or anyone else just yet. *Listen to me, Jaegar,* she said. *You drank from Suzanne-Alice –*

she's a Carrier, like me. Or at least a part-Carrier. You might have been tainted with Life's Blood; you need to stay calm. Fight your urges – please, Jaegar. Just try to stay calm, for me?

She gasped as she felt a hand wrap around her from behind. It was Jaegar, stalking silently behind her.

"Just a moment, Max," Jaegar smiled. "If I could borrow your daughter for a moment…"

He led her to a secluded part of the plane, pushing her behind the curtains, his mouth finding hers, devouring her as his passion found upon her lips its fullest expression. "Did you say something, Kalina?" He smiled, cat-like. "All I can hear is that pounding in your heart for me…the pounding of desire."

Kalina thought fast. If Jaegar did want her – the best thing she could do would be to convince him to drink from her, first. Her Life's Blood might well save him; it might turn him human. After all, it had done so before.

Blood Legacy: Pulse 6

"Do you want me, Jaegar?" Kalina gave him her most seductive look, widening her eyes as she stared into his face. "If you do, take me." She pushed back her hair, revealing her long, white neck.

Jaegar smiled as he fingered the soft, creamy skin. "Of course I do," he murmured. "But I want to enjoy you in so many other ways first..."

"Kalina!" Octavius broke in before Kalina had a chance to respond. She cursed silently as she looked up to find Octavius standing over them. "I wanted to inform you that you will be dining with me tonight – in Beverly Hills. I've telephoned the servants already – instructed them to prepare a sumptuous meal."

Kalina flashed back to the last time she had been to that mansion. Back then, Octavius had been arrogant, cruel – power-hungry. He had been her enemy, grown cold to human suffering by too many years on the job. She had almost forgotten that Octavius. But now, in his eyes, she saw him again.

"And the Carriers?" Kalina asked, hoping

Octavius would be stronger against the Blood than Jaegar. "We have to find them."

"Yes," Octavius said curtly, "we do." He turned to Jaegar. "You've always gotten in my way, Jaegar. Always gotten underfoot. I sired you, so I let you have your fun flirting, playing with my woman – but no more, Jaegar. Why she desires you as she does is beyond me; I *made* you, Jaegar – every ounce of blood in your veins is mine. But her heart wanders when you come calling. No more. You defied my orders once in keeping her from me; you will not defy me a second time. From this time forth, you will stop your quest for her. You are *my* offspring, Jaegar, and you will do as I command."

Jaegar scoffed. "I'm no newborn vampire," he said. "You can't tell me what to do. I'll fight you if I have to..."

"Fight your sire?" Octavius raised an eyebrow. "Fight a vampire more than twice your age with more abilities than you'll ever have? You fool – you wouldn't dare."

Blood Legacy: Pulse 6

Jaegar stepped forward, his stance threatening. He looked like a tiger who was getting ready to pounce. "I bet you I would," he growled. "You have no hold over me, Octavius."

Octavius smiled. "Oh, but I do." In a swift, graceful movement, he shot out a hand, catching Jaegar by the throat. He pushed him against the wall, staring at him with his enormous dark eyes. It took a moment for Kalina to realize what Octavius was doing.

"Octavius – *don't!*" she cried, but it was too late.

"You will no longer feel anything for Kalina," Octavius said. Jaegar's eyes were growing misty with the effects of the glamour. "You will no longer want her. You will no longer desire her. She will be nothing but a Carrier to you."

"No..." Jaegar was fighting it, fighting Octavius' words with every muscle of his being. "No, I love..." He was shaking violently – fighting the compulsion, trying so hard to cling to his love for her. And then his muscles went slack.

"Shut off your feelings," Octavius said. "Now!"

Jaegar's face was now serene – almost blank. He looked up at Kalina, but she saw no recognition there. No love. "Very well," he said simply and lightly. "What do you wish me to do with the Carrier, then?"

"Octavius, *no!*" Tears were falling down Kalina's face, but it was no use. Jaegar hardly seemed to recognize her at all.

"Now I can have you all to myself." Octavius shrugged.

"Kalina!" They were interrupted by Max. "Octavius needs to try to open the box. Perhaps he's old enough – he might be the one."

Kalina turned her face from her mother. "Just give us a second, Mom," she said, her voice shaking. She knew that sooner or later, she would have to admit what happened – but right now, she couldn't bear it. If Max gave her blood to either vampire, it would only make things worse. She was the only one who could feed Jaegar *or* Octavius.

"My sweet Kalina," Octavius went over to her. "All this time, I thought I only wanted your blood. Your delicious blood. To sample all to myself. But I want more than your blood, my darling. I have spent so long protecting Carriers, marrying them off to other vampires. I have served them all so well. But I want more."

"What are you talking about?" Kalina was trembling. "Don't you just want me – want to drink from me at last?" She held out one last, desperate hope that he would drink from her; that this would be enough to save him.

"I do want to drink from you," said Octavius. "But not *only* from you. There are so many Carriers out there – so many flavors – so much pleasure..." His eyes glimmered wickedly. "Why settle for one beautiful Carrier when I could take them all?"

"No, Octavius, no!" Kalina cried, but it was too late. The Octavius she had known – the Octavius she had loved – was gone.

kailin gow

PULSE continues in
Blood Rights - Book 7 of PULSE
2012

Brotherhood of Blood
(a PULSE Vampires Novel)
Available Now

Brotherhood of Blood is the first book in the Brotherhood of Blood Series About Octavius, The Greystone Brothers, the Vampire Consortium, and Octavius' army of vampire mercenaries.

Visit and Sign up for New Releases at:
http://kailingow.wordpress.com

kailin gow

From Author
Kailin Gow

the phantom diaries

What happens to the Phantom after the tragedy at the Paris
Opera House is the basis for this fantastic tale of The Phantom
Diaries, loosely based on Gaston Leroux's classic, *The Phantom
of the Opera*, but with a new tale and a modern twist. This new
series for older teens and young adults is told through the eyes of
18 year-old Annette Binoche, who lands a job at the New York
Metropolitan Opera House as a seamstress' assistant only to
become the lead singer of the Opera House, with the help of the
mysterious, yet highly-seductive Phantom.

**Now Available from
Author Kailin Gow**

dark memories (the phantom diaries, #2)

The evil presence has permeated every core of Annette Binoche's life, attempting to destroy everything and everyone she holds dear. Can she break free from its hold and regain the trust of her friends and family? Eric is forced to confront his past, while Annette is forced to decide on her future. Will it include Eric, Aaron or Chace? Or no one at all?

kailin gow

Wicked Woods

Briony had to move to Wicked Woods, Massachusetts to live
with her Great Aunt Sophie after her family disappears on
vacation. The woods at the edge of Aunt Sophie's inn are filled
with secrets and inhabitants both seductive and deadly. Among
them is a beautiful boy name Fallon who saves her one night in
the woods. As Briony gets closer to Fallon, she learns he has a
secret, as do most of the residents of Wicked Woods...

Want to Know More about the *PULSE Series*, Author Insight, Author Appearance, Contests and Giveaways?

Join the *PULSE Series* Official Facebook Fan Page at:

http://www.facebook.com/PULSEseries

Talk to Kailin Gow at:

http://kailingow.wordpress.com

and

on Twitter at: @kailingow

kailin gow

Want More Edgy books like *PULSE*?

visit

the EDGE

theedgebooks.com

Where you will find edgy books for teens and young adults that would make your heart pound, your skin crawl, and leave you wanting more...

Feed Your Reading Addiction

Sign up for news, book giveaways, author signings, ARC giveaways, promotions, specials, contests, job announcements, events, and more!

CPSIA information can be obtained at www.ICGtesting.com
Printed in the USA
LVOW11s1937270716

498005LV00003B/550/P